MY NAME IS EZRA

(The Thief On The Cross)

CYNTHIA THILLET

MY NAME IS EZRA

(The Thief On The Cross)

CYNTHIA THILLET

MY NAME IS EZRA (The Thief on the Cross)
Cynthia Thillet

© 2017 by Cynthia Thillet. All rights reserved

No part of this publication may be reproduced, stored in a retrieval system, or transmitted in any way by any means- electronic, mechanical, photocopy, recording, or otherwise- without the prior permission of the copyright holder, except as provided by USA copyright law.

ISBN 13: 978-1981388073
ISBN 10: 1981388079

Cover picture by Mike Somerville
-- *A retired United Methodist pastor, Mike started taking watercolor painting classes about seven years ago. He lives in Colorado Springs, Colorado, with his wife of 42 years, and can be reached on Facebook as J Michael Somerville.*

MY NAME IS EZRA *(THE THIEF ON THE CROSS)*

CYNTHIA THILLET

MY NAME IS EZRA

CHAPTERS

FOREWORD	11
PAIN	15
IN THE BEGINNING	21
THE FIRST TIME	27
MY SLING	31
THE END OF THE GOOD LIFE	37
GRANDFATHER	41
SLAVERY	47
MARINA	53
HORSES	61
THE PROPOSAL	65
ESCAPE	71
ON THE LOOSE	75
JOHN THE BAPTIST	79
DOWN BY THE SEA	89
MOM, ONCE MORE	95
THE SERMON ON THE MOUNT	101
THE WOMAN AT THE WELL	107
THE SEARCH	113
QUESTIONS	117
ENTRY INTO JERUSALEM	121
IMPRISONED	131

FIRST TRIAL	**135**
SECOND TRIAL	**143**
ANOTHER CELL	**149**
CARRYING THE CROSS	**155**
BACK TO THE PRESENT	**161**
EPILOGUE	**169**

MY NAME IS EZRA *(THE THIEF ON THE CROSS)*

CYNTHIA THILLET

MY NAME IS EZRA *(THE THIEF ON THE CROSS)*

FOREWORD

I started to write this book to answer a question that I had for a long time: "How did the thief on the cross know that Jesus had no sin, and how did he know there was a place to go after death?" This story is my way of answering that question. While a work of fiction, the events are based on the Biblical and historical events.

For the first chapter, I was able to visualize the actual events as they happened. When it was written I immediately sent if off to my four sisters and they requested more of the story. As I wrote, I sent them what I had written and their response was always the same, "I like it but I want more."

Their feedback was invaluable. The chapter where Ezra encounters Jesus came from a suggestion I received from them.

Other suggestions came from my co-workers, one of whom is Mike, a retired preacher. He suggested additions in the telling of John the Baptist.

I had a hard time finding a picture for the cover of my book. I searched the internet and none seemed just right. One week, Mike was telling us about some of his artwork he was selling to fund his mission trip. Until this time, I did not know he was an artist and could do watercolor. I asked him if he could do an art work for my cover. He agreed and I thank him for his original work.

Every day before I wrote I would pray about what I should write next. One day, while I was having "writer's block", during prayer time I heard God say, "Just start writing and I will give you the words". That day I wrote five pages. Another day I was ready to give up writing and God said, "If you don't write this book someone else will." Then I knew that this was a story that needed to be written.

I describe myself as a normal person who relies heavily on my relationship with Jesus. I am a wife, a mother of three, and grandmother of six. I work at Walmart. So, for God to choose me to write this book I am highly honored and give Him the glory.

I have written one other book called, Love Notes to My Husband (and Yours), which is based on love notes I wrote to my husband that he had saved. One day he presented me with them and we read them and laughed. I wanted to share them and now many of them are copied in this book.

"Ezra" has been a part of my life for over a year now. I have suffered with him, cried with him and rejoiced with him. I have seen him. My goal for this book is for the reader to be changed and know that no matter what they have done or have gone through, there is still hope.

God bless you all.

P.S. To Frieda, Melinda and Kris, "seesters" one, three and five, thank you for putting up with all my phone calls.

To Ray, my husband, you have put up with a lot and still give me the encouragement to be me.

To Patty, seester two, you believed in this project from the beginning and without you this book would be a mess.

CYNTHIA THILLET

MY NAME IS EZRA *(THE THIEF ON THE CROSS)*

PAIN

The centurion raises his arm high as he holds the spike at my wrist. "One," I count as his hammer hits hard on the spike. "Eeeaaah!" I scream involuntarily as the spike enters. I writhe trying to get away from the pain, but the ropes hold me in place. "Two." The hammer hits again. Deeper the spike goes. The pain is unbearable. I twist, and splinters from the wood dig into the lashes on my back. I thought the five lashes I received were the worst pain possible, but this is by far more than any person should have to bear. "Three." This time the spike digs into the wood jarring my whole body. "Four...five." Now my hand is pinned to the wood. Every movement sends pain down my arm. I try to move my fingers, but for what? I can't wipe the sweat from my face.

The soldier stands and stretches. As he moves to the other side of me, I can hear the gathering crowd. I can also hear groans as they try to imagine how it feels. Many are cheering, thankful that I am finally getting what I deserve. Those people are right. I am a thief.

He bends over pulling my arm out far to my left. I feel tearing in my wrist as he pulls on my arm placing my left hand in position to repeat the same torture. Again he raises the hammer, ready to strike. I brace myself knowing what is coming. Whack! He hits the spike, and it is the same horrible pain. I close my eyes to try and shield some of the torture, but it doesn't help. I look at the soldier's face, and it is stone cold. No emotion, no compassion. Apparently, he has done this before. I look hard at him, trying to figure what forces required him to have to do this. Maybe it was for the money, and maybe there were threats. Whatever the reason, I knew it wasn't his first time. He raises his hand again, and with the hit, I feel the spike pierce through and dig into the wood. Three more strikes and he is done.

I watch as the soldier moves to my left. There are two other men here being crucified with me. The one on my far left is Gestes. He is a thief also. I heard he would kill a man just for looking at him the wrong way. We hung out for a short time, but I didn't like his ways.

The man in the middle, now that is a different story. I don't know why He is here, but it must have been pretty bad. I can see his ribs showing through his severely lacerated skin. He must have done something really awful to have been whipped that badly. He has a crown of thorns shoved on his head causing streaks of blood to run down his face, which was already bleeding from where they had pulled out his beard. I wonder what crime he committed to deserve such punishment.

The soldier next goes to Gestes. I know the process now, but that doesn't make it any easier. I feel the pain all over as I hear the hammer hit the nail. Gestes curses loudly, and even from my distance, I can see his legs flailing. If his other hand were not already roped to the wood, he would have knocked out the soldier. With each pound, his curses get louder.

The soldier finished with him and moved to the man in the middle. Again the soldier raises his hammer high. Again the hammer comes down hard. He makes a noise but not like a scream—it was more a gasp. It was like he already accepted the pain before it happened. All the while, He looked steadily at the soldier. It was not a look of hate. It was almost like the look that a mother would give her child. He spoke nothing but his eyes said everything. I could almost hear him saying to the soldier, "Do what you have to do, I forgive you." I watched as the centurion hammered in his other hand. The man's look never changed, and the soldier couldn't turn his eyes away. As he finished, he rose, and I could see him raise his arms to wipe away the sweat but he also wiped away his tears.

For a bit, I am thankful that they have placed a small piece of wood at my feet so that I may lift my body off the wood and give my hands a short break from the pain searing through my arms. The relief only lasts a short while until a second soldier comes and grabs my feet. He removes what is left of my clothes. "NO!" I shout. He turns and with his back to me places my feet one on top of the other holding them tight. I look down and see a mallet held high in the air. With the loud thud of the hammer, I let out the most awful guttural scream I have ever heard. My feet were split open. A few more hits and I could no longer move my feet if I tried.

The soldiers moved on to Gestes. After seeing what happened to me, he knew what was coming I never saw such screaming and kicking. It took several guards to grab his feet. Shortly they did, and I saw his clothes go flying. I heard the hammer followed by more horrendous cursing. It seemed that up until this point Gestes really thought he would still find a way to escape.

They moved next to the man in the middle. He made not a sound as they took off his clothes. He seemed to almost help the soldier place his feet. They raised the hammer and let it go. He made only one loud involuntary groan as he grimaced. He just let them do what they had to do.

The next thing I knew there were men with ropes. This time they went first to the middle man. They looped the heavy ropes around the crossbars. With four men behind the cross and several in the front, they raised the cross. Slowly, at first, it rose; then faster as they got it in position over the ready dug hole. When it was in an upright position, it suddenly fell deep into the hole with a thud. I heard him cry out.

I was next. As the men raised me up, I could feel

my hands start to tear. I tried to push up with my feet to ease the pain, but then my feet felt like they were ripping in half. Every time I would push up, wood pieces would scrape the sores on my back. As I reached the peak, I tried to brace for the drop. It didn't help. My whole body screamed in pain. My mouth let the world know what my body felt.

Gestes knew by this time what was coming and there was no end to his cursing and screaming. Eventually, he must have figured less screaming and gyrating made less pain as his screaming subsided.

Our last humiliation was the boards they nailed over our heads. Jesus' read "Jesus Christ, King of the Jews." Gestes' read, "Thief and murderer." Mine read, "Thief and Run-away slave." As they were nailing my sign up, I started to think about my life and how I came to be here hanging for the entire world to see.

MY NAME IS EZRA *(THE THIEF ON THE CROSS)*

IN THE BEGINNING

My name is Ezra. I am the first and only son born to Binah and Chanoch. My mother wed my father when she was 14 years old. Her father, Omar, arranged the marriage to the son of a merchant when she was still a very young girl and at 13 she became betrothed to Chanoch Dysmas.

Binah's family lived in the small village of Jezreel. Her mother died in childbirth leaving her aunts and her father to care for her. Her father farmed the land of the Roman, Atticus, who lived in Jezreel. Binah was a great favorite of her father. He loved spoiling her with pretty robes and trinkets he just happened to come across. So, it was no surprise that when the day of the wedding celebration arrived, he threw her the biggest feast inviting everyone in the small village.

Everyone knew that Omar was a farmer, but no

one seemed to ask where he got the money for the feast. No one, not even Binah, knew that he borrowed so much money from Atticus. He promised that he would work more fields to pay back the money and for a while he did.

Nine months after the wedding I was born! What a celebration there was! Finally, there was a boy born in my grandfather's lineage. For the first few years, life was good. We lived in a small house in Jezreel near my father's shop. Some of my earliest memories were eating on the roof watching the sunset as the city folks strolled the streets. My mom and dad would laugh and talk of all that happened during the day. Often when the lights got low father would tell stories from the books of the law, and we would sit listening marveling at how God did such miracles and how quickly evil was punished.

My sister, Seleta, was born when I was nearly five. Mother had a hard time of it. This left her very weak for a while. It was then that I was expected to be the little man of the family. I had chores to do: sweeping, airing the rugs, anything to make things "easier for mom." Watching Seleta while mom made the bread or washed clothes became a regular chore. Things changed a lot.

There were fewer times where it was just Mom and Dad and me. They just didn't have time for me anymore.

Soon after the chores started so did my "schooling." Now, instead of the stories that Dad told being fun, they became a trial. They were part of the lessons I had to learn. I was slow to catch on. Numbers were especially hard for me until dad took me to work with him. He would let me sit with him under the huge tent waiting for people to shop. I loved seeing the crates piled high with birds of all sorts. On the other side were piles of material and skins. I watched as the people came in. They kept asking Dad lots of questions and then finally decided what to get. He took their coins, and I watched as he counted them as he placed them in his leather pouch. After the first time, I started counting with him. The coins were so shiny, and I longed to touch them. Dad must have noticed how my eyes lit up because when things got slow, he would open his leather bag and take out several coins. I learned to count really fast.

As a reward, Dad gave me one very small coin. I was so excited! I held that coin tight in my hand at first. Then I wanted to see it up close. I opened my hand, and the sun shone off it so brightly. The coin twinkled like a star when I moved my hand. I couldn't help staring at it. It was only my dad speaking that diverted my attention from the coin. He suggested we go across the road to the fruit stand and see what we could get with it. I was getting hungry and readily agreed. The fruit stand had so many choices: figs, pomegranates and grapes, but what caught my eye were the apples. They were so big and red. I could just imagine biting into one. I picked the biggest one and looked at my dad. He smiled and told me to give my coin to the shopkeeper. I looked at my shiny coin, and I looked again at the apple. I didn't want to give away my coin, but that apple looked so good, I finally gave it up.

We went back to the shop, and I sat happily eating my apple. It tasted as good as I imagined. The crisp sound it made as I bit into it and the sweet juicy flavors bursting in my mouth almost made losing my coin worth it. All too soon it was gone. The rest of the day I continued helping dad count the money but each time the coins went into the pouch I thought of mine and how pretty and sparkly it had been.

That night Dad told my mom what a good helper I

was and how quickly I learned to count. They decided that I could continue going on the days when my chores were done and when Mom wasn't too busy to watch Seleta all the time.

The next time I went, it was pretty much the same. Dad again noticed how hard I worked at learning my numbers, and I even tried adding the coins. They felt so cool in my hands and were so shiny. It was fascinating to me that I didn't feel like I was learning. This kind of learning was fun. Once again Dad gave me a coin. The joy of seeing the shine of the coin, feeling its coolness and knowing that that coin was mine was almost too overwhelming. This time Dad took me to the bread stand. Never had I seen so many different kinds of bread. There were loaves as big as my head, cheese rolls, and flat rolls but the one that caught my eye smelled so delicious. It was a honey roll as big as my hand. I looked at Dad, and he nodded and instantly I knew I had to give up my coin to get this treat. With Dad's eye on me, I slowly opened my hand and gave the man the coin. The sweet roll was great, but as soon as it was gone, I had nothing.

CYNTHIA THILLET

MY NAME IS EZRA *(THE THIEF ON THE CROSS)*

THE FIRST TIME

I continued going to the shop with Dad from time to time. Each time I got a coin, and we went to get a small treat. Parting with that coin was harder each time. I began understanding what coins were for and sometimes I would pick something that my coin could not buy, and dad would not let me have it. I knew better than to argue with my dad.

One day, the shop was really busy. Dad gave me my coin as usual. I admired it and watched how the sun shone on it making reflections on the tent wall. Oh, how I wanted to keep it. To my surprise, instead of Dad going with me to get a treat, and since the fruit stand was so close and I was "getting older," he let me go alone. I figured he was too busy.

The fruit stand was also busy. When I walked up the shopkeeper had just greeted some longtime friends. I decided to choose an apple that day. They looked extra big, and I hadn't had one in quite a while. I waited for a short time, but the shopkeeper just kept right on talking. I picked up my chosen apple, and still he ignored me. I held my coin in my hand hesitating about what to do. Then it hit me: I could have my apple and my coin! I slowly walked away, and no one knew what happened. I walked around to the back of the tent and took a bite of my apple as I held my coin in the sun.

Before I went back to my dad's shop, I twisted the coin in my belt and showed Dad that I was able to get the apple all by myself. He looked very pleased.

That night Dad was talking to Mom telling her how proud he was of me but that he wished I was a little older because business was starting to be very good. They decided to hire an older boy to help who knew how to count and who was good with the people. That is how Abir came to be. The next time I came in, he was there, and there were a lot more people around. I did my best to be helpful just like Abir was. Abir was 12 years old, almost a man but he still wore a shorter robe. He was about a head taller than I was and had shoulder-length hair. What I really liked was that he carried a sling in his belt. He told me he used it to scare away animals as he walked to work. Often he had vicious, barking dogs come after him. But he used that sling and scared them off. I was impressed. Sometimes, when we had finished our lunches, he let me try it out. I wasn't very good at all at first, and Abir laughed at me. I remember how proud I was the first time I hit the post. Then I really wanted a sling. He showed me how I could use a small bit of leather and rope and make my own sling.

For the next few weeks, I tried to make my own. I asked Dad for some rope and Mom for small pieces of cloth. Then I carefully tied a loop for my thumb and placed the cloth in the middle of the long rope. I whirled it around my head just like I saw Abir do. The loop broke, and the cloth flew off. The next few times I made one it broke on the first shot. The more I tried, the more upset I got when one failed. Abir said it was probably the rope that was too thin or the cloth was too old. I asked for help, and Dad and Mom were too busy to help me. I kept trying, but my materials just didn't work.

One day I wanted to work on my sling and mom

made me watch Seleta. She didn't want to sit at all. Each time I gave her a toy she would play with it a minute and then get up and toddle away looking for Mom. Mom was baking bread, and it was too dangerous to have a little one underfoot, so I was stuck. Finally, I lost patience with her and slapped her a good one and made her sit. She wailed so loud that I could hear the neighbors hollering to Mom asking what had happened. Mom was already by my side. She grabbed my ear and dragged me to my room. I was ordered to stay till Dad got home and one of the neighbor ladies who felt sorry for Seleta sat and watched her while Mom finished up.

When Dad got home, I heard him and Mom talk a minute. When he came into my room, he had his knife-sharpening strap in his hand. He took me out back of the house and proceeded to show me what Seleta must have felt when I slapped her. I cried for a while and was red for hours. Never did I want to feel that again. I imagine the neighbors were smugly satisfied. Mom was appeased, Seleta smiled, and to Dad, it was over and done with.

MY NAME IS EZRA *(THE THIEF ON THE CROSS)*

MY SLING

After the first time I came back with my apple, Dad let me go by myself all the time. I ventured all through the marketplace deciding what I could get. After I found out how easy it was to get my apple, I looked for a merchant that was busy and just quietly helped myself to what I wanted. After a bit, I had a small pile of beautiful coins that twinkled and jingled when I shook them. I took them out only when I knew I was alone. One day on my excursion, I was looking for a pouch to put them in when I saw hanging high on a peg the most perfectly made sling. It was too far out of reach to take like I took the apple and it cost a lot more than the few coins that I was able to put away. I grabbed a pouch and thought about how I would get that sling all the way back to the shop. Because of the many customers, my longer absences were never noticed.

A few weeks later, a very well known rich widow came into the shop. Dad noticed her immediately as she walked toward the material. Abir was showing some doves to a young couple, so he handed me the money pouch and the money he was counting and told me to count it and put the money in. It was quite heavy. In my hand were several coins including one large one. I thought of the sling in the shop. I quickly put the smaller coins in the pouch and wrapped the larger one in my sash. Surely Dad wouldn't miss one coin. At that time Abir came over to deposit the coins from the sale of the doves, and I handed him the pouch.

When I got my coin from Dad, I went straight to the merchant that had the sling. Proudly I handed him the big coin, and he even gave me coins back! I hid the sling under my robe and went to get a fig.

Before we left the shop that night, dad counted the money as he always did. Then he counted it again making a lot of "harrumph" noises. He ordered Abir to make sure I got home. When we left, he was crawling all over the floor.

That night I practiced with my sling and hit the

post almost all the time. It was wonderful. Dad and Mom never questioned me about the sling. I guess they just thought I got really good at making them. If they had looked at it up close, they would have known better.

The next time I went to the shop, Abir was gone. I asked Dad where he was and he told me he couldn't have a thief working for him. I didn't make a comment. I should have because Abir was a good worker. I felt a little guilty but stealing had now become a pattern in my life and it became an easy means to get what I wanted.

My life became a lot busier. I started Hebrew school and Mom had another baby. Ruth was a good baby and didn't require quite as much watching as Seleta. Even so between schooling and watching my younger siblings I had very little time to myself. I went to the shop as much as mom could spare me. I became quite a good helper, and my little stash of coins continued to grow. I became very good at finding shops that were busy or where the keeper was very talkative. Only when Dad went with me was I forced to pay for my snack.

When I did get a few hours free, I would take my sling and go target hunting. The first time I shot a rabbit I was so excited. We had often had rabbit for meals at home. I especially enjoyed those meals. I triumphantly took the rabbit home to show my mom. I pictured how its fur would make such warm slippers on the cold nights. That would have been so nice. Dad and Mom were both very proud, and right away dad set out to skin the rabbit. I watched as he carefully sharpened his gleaming silver knife. Then with a quick slit up the center of the belly, he opened the rabbit. He doused it with cornmeal to soak up the juices and proceed to carefully peel the skin back. It just seemed to pull right off leaving the naked rabbit lying there. I watched as he expertly took out the entrails. I figured that anyone with a good knife could do it. It looked easy. Momma took the skin exclaiming how nice a hat it would make for little Ruth. I told her I wanted it for my slippers, but she said my old ones were fine. I started to protest, but as soon as I opened my mouth, my dad gave me that horrible look.

The next time I brought home a rabbit, Dad was not home, and Mom was busy outside with the washing. I decided to clean the rabbit myself. I took out the knife and the sharpening stone and just as Dad did I sharpened it. I got out the cornmeal and the cutting board, laid my rabbit on his back just as dad did, and slit open the rabbit's belly. It was easy! I carefully doused the flowing liquids with cornmeal and proceeded to pull off the skin. I managed quite nicely. I felt so proud. I was just getting the last of the skin off when in walked Mom and Dad. I happily held up the rabbit skin thinking how proud they should be of me. I was drastically wrong. Mom was so scared of what could have happened with a young boy and a knife. Dad was so mad. He let me know in no uncertain terms how wrong it was for me to use his knife and with no supervision. Then he proceeded to drag me by my ear and got the switch, and I felt how wrong he thought I was.

CYNTHIA THILLET

MY NAME IS EZRA *(THE THIEF ON THE CROSS)*

THE END OF THE GOOD LIFE

Inside I was so proud. I used a knife expertly and began to see how having a knife could open new challenges for me. I knew that I could never get my own knife from my parents. Somehow I had to get that knife. I counted up all the coins that I had saved, and it wasn't nearly enough to get the kind of knife I needed. I thought of ways I could steal the knife, but they were not kept in locations that I could get to. The only way I could figure to get it was to get the money from Dad's pouch. I knew this was going to be a huge challenge. Since Abir left, Dad rarely set his pouch down. The only time I saw him leave it behind was when wealthy buyers distracted him.

One day not too long after I decided how to get the money, our wealthiest shopper came in. Dad was so excited because he just came across some exotic purple fabric. He was in such a hurry to greet her he left the pouch behind. I watched as he started telling her about the new fabric. I eyed the pouch and quickly untied the string. I reached in and pulled out enough to buy my knife. I started tying it back up, and there was Dad. "It was you, not Abir, who stole the money! Just you wait." He snarled in such a voice that I had never heard. He started coming toward me, and I ran toward the back of the tent. At that point, he remembered the rich lady in the front and grabbed the fabric instead. I didn't look back but ran as fast as I could. I didn't know if he was following me. In my haste, I knocked over a pile of fabric and apparently the lantern. I heard a crash as I slipped under the edge of the tent.

I hurried to the knife shop and tried to purchase the knife. The shopkeeper didn't want to sell it to me since I was so young, but I told him I chipped my dad's knife when I was throwing it at the ground, so he sent me there with my hard earned money to buy a new one. It was a good story, and I soon had my knife. I was ecstatic and scared. I knew there would be a huge punishment when Dad got home, but until then I had my knife. The punishment would be worth it.

As I hurried home, I heard shouting back toward the shop, but I didn't want to face Dad so soon afterward. Maybe, I thought, a little time would cool his temper. When I reached home Mom questioned me why I came home alone and early. I just told her I wasn't feeling well and she sent me to bed with a little broth. I must have fallen asleep because I was awakened by loud wailings. I walked out quietly to find out what happened and there were many of the town folk in the house all speaking at once. "He went back in…," "Saved some birds…," "fire spread fast… " "fine fabric…," "pole fell…," "Can't believe he is dead…," "He was such a fine man…," and then, "They tried to pull him out but the fire was too hot, and he was trapped."

Mom was crying, the babies were crying, and I was thinking that this was my fault. That is when they saw me. Mom ran to me and threw her arms around me and cried all the more. I cried because Mom was crying. Then it dawned on me that nobody knew that I caused the fire and nobody knew that I stole the money and I had a knife and I wasn't going to get beat.

CYNTHIA THILLET

MY NAME IS EZRA *(THE THIEF ON THE CROSS)*

GRANDFATHER

After Dad was buried things changed really fast. We could no longer afford to live in our home. Grandfather Omar took us in. He lived in a small hut in the countryside near the fields he worked in. Grandfather had aged a lot since I last saw him. He was a frail man, and though not extremely old, he looked very old, with weatherworn skin and a balding head. He walked with a limp and was hunched over.

Although he was pleased to have us come, when he thought we weren't looking, I could tell something was going on inside. He would put his head in his hands and groan. He wasn't home much. He left to work in the fields before dawn and rarely showed up till after dinner. Momma tried to do her part by washing and taking in mending.

The years we spent with Grandfather flew by.

When I wasn't attending to my schooling, helping Mom or watching Seleta and Ruth, I would spend all day in the fields far from home. There I would perfect my aiming with my sling. I caught many rabbits. I learned to build a fire and cook the rabbit. I tried to save the skin of the rabbit, but it never worked. The skin just dried stiff and smelly. There was a pond nearby where I practiced fishing, and once in a while, I caught one.

At night when Grandfather did make it home early, he would often bring a piece of material for Mom or some ties for her hair and a sweet treat for us kids. Then after the meal, he would tell us stories. Mostly they were funny stories from when Mom was little, but once in a while, he would tell us stories about old kings and long ago. My favorite was when David, a small boy, killed the giant. I knew I could have done that. I often dreamed that I was out killing lions and giants.

Sometimes we had visits from relatives. I enjoyed the change, and Momma always was so cheerful when they came. One visitor that surprised me was my dad's brother, Chalev. His wife died in childbirth, and he had never remarried. He lived by the sea where he fished and mended nets. He especially loved playing with Seleta and Ruth. He always lectured me about my schooling and how I should apply myself more to my studies. His visits became a regular thing. He would bring fish for dinner, and Ruth and Seleta would run to meet him. Often I would catch Momma and him having private conversations. Sometimes I would catch bits of it like Momma saying, "I couldn't," or he would say, "they need a father." Then they would see me and stop abruptly. It was apparent they had some kind of connection that an young man couldn't or didn't want to see.

A month after my thirteenth birthday, we were having a late dinner expecting Grandfather anytime. It had been extremely hot that day, so the fresh grapes and smoked fish were perfect. We all kept looking at the doorway for Grandfather, but he didn't show. This posed no alarm, as he had been late before. We were put to bed, and he still hadn't shown up. By morning when he wasn't back Mom was alarmed. Before noon, we found out the reason for his absence. They had found his body in the field overcome by the heat. Atticus came that same day and let Momma know the state of Grandfather's affairs. He said he would be back to settle the account "one way or the other." Three days later, surrounded by all the relatives, Grandfather Omar was laid in a pauper's field. None of them had enough money to pay off his debt.

A week later, Atticus was back. The house we were staying in belonged to him. We had to go. The debt had to be paid. Mom sent me to watch the kids outside while they talked. When he left Momma came out crying.

She said that everything was settled and it was the only way. The way. I would go live with Atticus for seven years to pay off Grandfather's debt, and then I would be free with a small amount of money to start life. Momma would marry Chalev, and he would take her and the kids with him to the sea. All I could say was, "No, Momma, no!" and, "I hate you!" over and over. She kept saying that there was no other way. Atticus wouldn't take the whole family and besides that Dad's brother couldn't afford me.

Momma had a small ceremony three days later. That same day a servant of Atticus came to get me. I had a parcel I insisted on packing with my extra clothes. Inside were my knife, my sling and my small bag of coins. I gave Seleta and Ruth a hug like I would any other day. They were too young to really understand what was happening. I shook Chalev's hand and gave Mom a hug. I was still furious, but even I knew that this could be my last time seeing her. Inside I wanted to cry like a baby, but outside I shut off my emotions.

CYNTHIA THILLET

MY NAME IS EZRA *(THE THIEF ON THE CROSS)*

SLAVERY

The ride to Atticus' house was not overly long, and by late afternoon we were there. It was the largest house that I had ever seen and nicely situated on a hill. Under one side of it was the stable that housed the horses. Chickens and goats roamed the yard. In the stable to the side was a small room that was big enough for two beds. One was mine, and the other belonged to Ole Shem. My job was to learn from Shem how to care for the animals and clean the stable.

That first day I didn't have any chores, so I was allowed to roam the area. I took my sling and walked about. In the distance, I could see the vast fields where I could picture Grandfather working along with the others. Near the house was a well where they drew water and where I would have to fetch the water for the animals. In the yard were women weaving rugs and churning butter.

Around them, young children were alternately watching and then running off to play. There were small buildings a short distance from the main house that must have housed a few servants.

When I returned, my meal was sitting by my bed. I was advised to get to sleep early because the morning chores started early.

They did. While it was still dark, Ole Shem woke me up. My first task was to fetch water for all the animals. Shem didn't take any lip. In that way, he reminded me of my dad. I lost track of how many trips I made to the well to get the water to fill the troughs. My shoulders ached, and I told Shem, and he just told me how I would get used to it soon enough.

After watering was done, came feeding the animals and cleaning the stalls. This was not only backbreaking, but the smell was horrible. After a while, I think I got used to the smell, or I started smelling like the barn. I wasn't sure which.

Ole Shem kept pushing me to be faster. For a young guy like me who was used to doing very little hard work, this was not easy. By the time I had cleaned the stalls, I was ready for a break. We had a quick breakfast and I thought I was done but Ole Shem wasn't done with me yet.

Next, I had to gather the eggs and make sure none of the chickens got taken in the night by some predatory animal. Counting the chickens was not easy. They had free reign over a good part of the yard. It seemed to take forever to locate all the chickens and goats for counting.

Shem helped me with my work for a while until I got the hang of it. He was old, but that didn't slow him down. As I got stronger, I was able to finish those tasks before noon.

Shem's main job was to care for the horses. I envied him when he brushed them. They would nicker as he crooned to them while he brushed them and checked them over. Then, while I was cleaning their stalls, he was on their backs exercising them.

Shem also milked the goats. I thought this was fascinating. I never considered where my milk came from before. To think that these playful, mischievous animals supplied our cheese and milk was amazing. Shem caught me watching him milk the goats and called me over. I thought he was going to holler at me but he had me to sit next to him. Then he showed me how he tugged on the udders to get a good stream. I wasn't very good but it was fun. The goats were so comical and seemed glad that the extra burden was being lifted from them

When I got better at milking the goats, that also became my job. When morning chores were done we had a break. For the first months, morning chores lasted till noon. We would have our meal of cheese, bread and whatever fruit there was. Then Shem would take a nap. I did also until I got stronger. After napping, there was a bit of free time until evening chores. During this time I would take my sling and roam the farm.

Evening chores were almost the same as in the morning but fortunately, I didn't have to clean the stalls.

I was so busy in my new life that I had little time to think of my past life. When I did, I would blame my grandfather for getting so far into debt and my mother for leaving me behind. It never came to mind that my

MY NAME IS EZRA *(THE THIEF ON THE CROSS)*

situation could have been all my fault.

CYNTHIA THILLET

MY NAME IS EZRA *(THE THIEF ON THE CROSS)*

MARINA

One day, when I took the milk and eggs to the kitchen, a girl a little younger than me opened the door. She had long dark hair and the bluest eyes I have ever seen. I could hardly squeak out a "Hi" to her as I handed her the eggs. She took them and came back for the milk. I found my voice long enough to ask her name.

"Marina," she answered. "I saw you with your sling."

Then she was called away.

I began looking for Marina when I went out to gather water. I would see her sitting and sewing near the other women and occasionally she would look up and smile. If her mother noticed she would get a nudge and go quickly back to her sewing. Something inside of me heated up whenever she noticed me. Once in a while I would be gathering water in the afternoon and Marina would come with her pitcher for water. Her nose would twitch and then she would smile. She barely spoke but her smile was enough. She knew she was being watched.

I asked Shem about Marina and found out she was Atticus' youngest daughter. He warned me to stay away from her but that just urged a young kid like me to try harder. At this time also, I noticed my body changing. Ole Shem was the only one I could talk to and he explained what was happening. He even showed me how to shave even though he let his beard grow at will.

I became more interested in my appearance and asked Shem how I could get new clothes. I had grown a lot in the first year. About a week later, I was given a used robe and we were allowed to go to town and get other necessary items. While Shem was finishing the purchase, I went out to survey the other shops. One, in particular, was selling fragrant spices and soaps. I quickly grabbed a bottle and went back to find Shem.

One morning, just before sunrise, I was walking in the yard to get an idea where I might find the rascally chickens for my count. As usual, I had my sling on me with a few stones ready to go. The chickens were making a lot of raucous as I approached. This was unusual since they had not yet spied me with their breakfast. Soon I could see the reason for their alarm. Slinking along in the weeds was a fox eyeing out our fattest and slowest chicken. I hurriedly let a stone fling in his direction. I was rewarded with an ear piercing, "Yowl," I let another stone go and he moved no more. The noise brought Ole Shem over. When he approached, I was standing over the fox's carcass contemplating what I would do with the fur.

"Well done," he said, "Atticus will hear of this." Then he picked up the fox body and headed for the main house.

When Shem returned, I was told to clean up before evening chores for I would be dining in the main house. I would have preferred to keep the fox skin but no chores and a chance to be with Marina almost made up for it.

I scrubbed my skin till it was raw and put on my cleanest robe that I had doused with my fragrance. As I walked over, I could hardly contain all the excitement that was going on in my body.

Atticus greeted me at the door with a firm handshake. He told me how the neighbors have been losing chickens and what a great service this was to his family. We proceeded to the dining area where all his children and grandchildren were gathered. To my delight I was seated across from Marina. The food was like none I have ever seen. They had roasted a goat and cooked the most amazing variety of legumes and breads. They had a huge platter of fruits and cheeses. The most amazing thing was the wine. I never had wine before. It was fruity, a bit sweet and a bit tart. Its aroma reminded me of the fruit stands on a hot summer day. When I tasted it, it warmed my insides. After a half a glass my senses became sharper and I felt more relaxed. Once during dinner I was reaching for a piece of fruit at the same time Marina was. Our hands touched and it was like a bolt of lightning going through me. I drew my hand back quickly. As I looked up Marina gave me a very big smile.

I told the story of how hard I had worked to be able to kill the fox. Marina was so excited that she asked her father if I could show her how to use the sling. To my surprise it was agreed upon if her chores and studying were done and I had time between my chores.

After dinner, while Atticus was walking me out he stepped into a side room for a moment. At the door he pressed a large coin into my hand and told me how grateful his wife was to now have something to warm her shoulders on the cold nights.

In the morning a few days later, I met Marina at the well. She said she would have time later that day if I were free. I instantly agreed and we settled for after lunch.

Marina and I met at the well. She had her five-year-old nephew, Marcus, with her. Her mother insisted on him accompanying her. Marcus was a blessing to have along. He was very inquisitive and loved my story of how I killed the fox. I exaggerated a bit and Marina laughed. Her laugh had to have been the prettiest sound I had ever heard. As we walked, I told again how hard it was for me to learn to use the sling.

I settled on a field out of view from the house that had a few trees in it and a small pond nearby. I showed her how to gather the perfect stones and even Marcus seemed to enjoy trying to find the right ones. After we each had a handful, I loaded one in my sling. I spun my sling in the air and right before I let it fly I glanced at her. The sun was making her hair look like black glass, her eyes matched the sky and her lips were as red as an apple. She was beautiful. My stone went flying way off course. She giggled and Marcus laughed uproariously. The second time I stayed focused and knocked a small twig off the nearby tree. Now they were impressed.

I carefully showed Marina how to swing her arm, so she got the right spin on the sling. She was not very good but I let her think she was. Marcus wanted to try so I let him but the sling was too long and dragged the grass. He quickly lost interest and went to chase grasshoppers.

Once Marina got a feel for the spin of the sling, I showed her how to flick her wrist to let it go. The first hardly went a few feet. The second went farther but off to the side. The rest went helter-skelter in all directions. I couldn't help but laugh. She would make the funniest face and then let out a small shriek. Before long we were both laughing hysterically.

When the sun started to set, we headed back. Marina slipped and I grabbed her hand. She smiled and didn't let go until the house came into view. As we got near the house, I spied a rabbit. I quickly set up and hit the rabbit first shot. Marina let out a cry and ran for the rabbit. Marcus and I quickly followed. I showed her that the rabbit never felt anything. She felt its warmth and the soft fur. I told her rabbit soup would be quite tasty and warm mittens would be nice. She carried the rabbit to the house like it was having a funeral. I left her and hurried to do my chores.

For a few years, life settled into a near routine. I knew that if I hurried through my chores I would have more free time. This meant that after lunch I would have a few hours of time to do as I pleased. On the times when Marina was free, we would go out to the field always accompanied by Marcus. She was full of life and the time we had together went by fast. She would share how she spent her days and I would tell of my past life. They seemed like so long ago now. I would tell her about my dad and mom, Seleta and Ruth but when I talked about them, it was like talking about someone else's family. I was still very hurt for what they did to me but when I was with Marina I was almost glad that I was sent away.

CYNTHIA THILLET

MY NAME IS EZRA *(THE THIEF ON THE CROSS)*

HORSES

The horses on the farm intrigued me. I asked Ole Shem about them. They acquired them from Egyptians that brought them up for sale. Here they were taken care of until the Roman guard needed them. Most had to be brushed and ridden regularly to stay in top condition. Marina and her father went out nearly every week to ride the horses together. She looked so beautiful with her raven hair flowing behind and her bright smile. She looked so free. I also wanted to feel that free.

The other horses were used for chariot racing. Shem would take six horses at a time and harness them together and then attach their harnesses to a small riding chariot. Then Shem would climb in the chariot and ride it around a track. He would not take the horses around very fast as he explained that he was training them to act as a team.

Shem was in charge of making sure they stayed in top health. Various members of the family often took them for rides in the morning, and on their return they need to be brushed and checked. I begged Shem to let me help him brush them. As I grew older, I was taller and stronger and finally he let me help him brush them.

They were magnificent beasts. At first I was a bit timid with them and they with me. Shem soon found out I was serious with them and he allowed me to brush them during my free time. After that I made sure I had free time. Shem saw how much I enjoyed being around the horses. One afternoon after nap time he asked if I would like to ride one. He said that there were two that hadn't been ridden in a few days and said it would be good for the horses. He showed me how to blanket and saddle the horse. Then he showed me how to mount and then guide the horse.

We walked them out of the corral. I wanted to go fast but I didn't want to ruin things. I obeyed everything Ole Shem said. On the way home, he allowed us to gallop. It was everything I had imagined. That night I dreamed of one day taking off on my own, free to do and go anywhere. Things must have gone well because the next time Shem needed an extra rider he asked me to go.

CYNTHIA THILLET

MY NAME IS EZRA *(THE THIEF ON THE CROSS)*

THE PROPOSAL

One afternoon, while Shem was still napping, I saw Marina at the well. I told her I had to show her something. I knew she liked to ride the horses but I believed she never got to brush them. I brushed one and she laughed at how they nickered at me. Then she wanted to try. She brushed in short choppy strokes and the horse whinnied. I got behind her and took her hand and showed her how to do the long firm strokes and the horse calmed down.

I could smell the fragrance in her hair she must have read my thoughts. She slowly turned around and was eye to eye with me. For a moment we said nothing; then she licked her lips and I kissed her. At that moment her mother called and she was gone.

Suddenly I could picture my future. As soon as my seven years were up, I would marry Marina and we could live on the farm. I would be the head foreman and live in the main house and we would have lots of children. It was perfect.

I wanted Marina to know how serious I was so I decided to buy her a gold armband. I asked Shem if I could go to town with him the next time he went. I told him I needed a change of scenery. I took all the money I had saved over the years and hid my pouch in my robe. While Shem was picking up things he needed, I went to the goldsmith and chose a beautifully etched gold armband. I showed the man all my money and told him of beautiful Marina and my plans to marry her. He must have noticed my desperation because he took all my money and told me it would be enough.

I must have danced on the way back to find Shem. He noticed something was up right away. I couldn't hide the grin that must have made my whole countenance shine. He asked what had happened and I told him I just needed to get away for the day. I don't think he believed me but I couldn't tell him the truth because of what he thought of Marina and me.

When Marina turned fourteen, her times with me

had dwindled. She was now "marrying age." That meant we had to wait till her parents were busy before we could get together. After I kissed her I was not really sure what her reaction would be. I waited for her to ask me if I was free. I made sure I was and she came prepared with a picnic lunch. This was a good sign.

We escaped with just the two of us. We strolled hand in hand down by the pond and set up in the shade of some olive trees. As we sat, I began.

"In one year I will be free to do as I want. I will no longer be a slave. I want to marry and have children. I want to live on a farm and raise horses. It would be so wonderful. I want that farm to be this farm and I want to marry you."

She made not a sound as I made my speech, so I continued.

"Marina, if you love me half as much as I love you we would be so happy together. Marina, Do you love me?"

Finally she spoke. "Yes, I believe I do, but are you sure you love me."

At this I pulled out the golden armband. Marina's eyes lit up and she slid the band on her arm above her elbow.

"It is beautiful! Yes, I do love you."

She leaned over and kissed me and I pulled her into my arms. We lay in a lover's embrace until we realized that we had to hurry back.

As we parted she had a troubled look on her face. "What will my father say?"

"I will talk to him," I said confidently.

Then she was gone.

The next day I put on my best clothes and walked up to the house. I asked to speak with Atticus. He was in his office counting his money. He stood and told me that I was doing a fine job caring for the animals. This gave me confidence and I began telling him how I would love to continue working for him after my time was up. This seemed to please him so I continued. I told him how I enjoyed my outings with Marina and had grown very fond of her. I told him I had asked her to marry me and she had agreed. I told him how we could live with him and raise our family close by. Then I asked his blessings on our betrothal.

As I spoke, his face went from pleased to hard. I talked faster to convince him of my sincerity. When I was finished his face was red with anger.

Then he spoke.

"No! This cannot be. You are a Hebrew. Marina is Roman. She will not marry a Hebrew. Furthermore, she is promised to her cousin. You may not see her again. To ensure this does not happen. I am sending you to the far fields to finish out your time. I am sending Marina away for a week and in that time you will be taken to live in the far quarters with the rest of the field workers. Now leave this house and don't ever mention or think of this idiotic scheme again."

He would not hear another word from me.

I left stunned, angry and heartbroken. Now what hope did I have? I could no longer be around the animals I grew to enjoy. I would have to work under the hot sun like my grandfather. I would no longer be able to see my beautiful Marina. I could not picture life here without seeing Marina, and without being able to ride the horses.

I had to get away. As I worked at my chores, I began to plot my escape. I no longer had any money. I knew I could survive off the land. I was still a slave so I would have to go far away and fast. I needed a horse. That was the easy part. I also needed money and I knew now where Atticus kept it.

MY NAME IS EZRA *(THE THIEF ON THE CROSS)*

ESCAPE

I now had a plan. The next day I went on as if nothing had happened. I saw a carriage at the house and knew Marina was leaving. She looked sad but resigned. I stared, unable to take my eyes off of her. Even in her sadness she was so beautiful. I watched until she was out of sight.

That night as I waited for Ole Shem to fall asleep, I decided that I would head east toward the sea. I figured if they tried to find me they would think that I would head toward the ocean. I heard there was good fishing on the sea and I knew the game would be quite plentiful. I would be fine there. I just needed a few items to shelter me and I would be fine.

After Shem had been sleeping for a while, I got up and gathered my few belongings. I headed to the horses and chose the biggest and I thought the fastest. I prepared him for the long ride and tied my pack onto his saddle. I walked outside and circled the house to make sure there wasn't anybody still up.

I went through the front door. There was no sound, so I continued to where I had seen Atticus counting the money. The light from the window gave me just enough light so that I could look around and not make any noise. Finally I found the money and took enough to just about double what I spent on Marina's armband. Some coins fell but I had all I needed, so I left them and hurried out.

As I approached the horse, I heard a shout coming from the house. It would take them a short while before they found out what was going on and to find out who stole the money. Very quietly and quickly I lead the horse out of the corral. As soon as I thought it was safe, I mounted and headed toward the ocean. I don't know how far behind the search party was or even if they were following me. After a short while I found a rocky area and turned the horse around and we headed east.

When I got on more stable ground, I urged the horse to go faster. I knew I had to put a lot of distance between the farm and me. I rode fast and hard all the rest of the night. By early morning I came upon a hollow in the hillside with grass all around. I let the horse rest and eat while I got some sleep. As I drifted off to sleep, I tried to plan what I was going to do. I needed shelter. I thought of my mother. My last thoughts were of Marina. What was she thinking? Did she miss me?

I slept till mid-afternoon and quickly caught a rabbit to eat and started again on my way. I didn't know where I was going. I had no plans.

CYNTHIA THILLET

MY NAME IS EZRA *(THE THIEF ON THE CROSS)*

ON THE LOOSE

One night while I was camping out, a band of men came up to me. I had a fire going and was smoking some meat for the next day. They were a very rough group of three men. The leader was named Gestes. He demanded I feed them and they took over my campfire. They passed around a skin of wine and asked me to have some. It tasted of vinegar. They asked me about my horse. I told them that I had just purchased it and was riding it home. The more wine they drank the more loosely they talked. They were bragging about the people they killed and the loot they pillaged. They invited me to join up with them and I just laughed.

As the fire died down so did the talk and I was soon fast asleep.

When I awoke, my horse was gone. Fortunately I had a habit of sleeping with my knife and sling, so I still had those.

At first I thought that this was a bad thing but because I was nearing a town, I decided it could be a good thing. The horse served my purpose and allowed me to get far away quickly. Now it would have made me very visible since Romans were the ones who rode horses.

In town, I decided to get cleaned up and replenish some of my supplies. The things I needed were not easily stolen and I still had money, so I purchased new sandals and a tarp for the cold nights. I saw a fruit stand and helped myself to an apple.

I noticed some Romans on horses in the street and quickly ducked out of site. I didn't want to take any chances. In the bathhouse I heard men talking of the Roman guard. They said there were looking for a prized horse that was stolen by a runaway slave.

I left town shortly after that heading east. I heard the river was that way and figured that might be a safe place to stay. It would have plenty of game and water and probably a well-sheltered spot.

MY NAME IS EZRA *(THE THIEF ON THE CROSS)*

I had no place to go, so I took my time and stayed off the main road. I rested when I was tired, ate when I caught food and walked when the sun was not hot.

CYNTHIA THILLET

MY NAME IS EZRA *(THE THIEF ON THE CROSS)*

JOHN THE BAPTIST

One day while I was preparing to cook my meal a man came walking up. He was a very robust looking man dressed in camel skin with a leather belt at his waist. He introduced himself as John. I invited him to eat with me and he said he only ate locusts and honey.

"How odd," I thought.

Then he pulled some locusts out of his pouch and offered me some. I shuddered but didn't want to offend him, so I closed my eyes and popped one in. Surprisingly they were quite tasty. They had a nice pleasing crunch with a gentle sweetness of honey.

"Actually they are quite good. I believe from the looks of you they must be quite good for you too. However, I still prefer my rabbit. At least you can rest by my fire. You do look like you could use a rest."

I proceeded to cook my rabbit. John looked at me and then made up his mind.

"Yes, I can use a rest. I have had a very long yet blessed day."

As we were sitting around the fire, me gnawing on my rabbit leg and him popping locusts, I couldn't help but ask him further about this unusual lifestyle.

"There is something very unusual about you, and I can sense that it is not only how you dress and eat. You seem to have something about you that I can't quite place. Please, tell me what it is."

"It is a long story and I must start at the beginning. If you are willing to listen, I will tell you."

"The night is young and the fire is hot so please tell."

So he began.

"When my parents were very old, God told my father that he would have a son named John. He didn't believe God, so God took away his voice. While I was in my mother's womb, her niece came to visit. Her niece,

Mary, was but a very young lady and she too was pregnant. My mother said I leaped in her womb. You see, she was a virgin yet pregnant!"

"Impossible!" I declared.

"Yes, impossible; but nothing is impossible for God. She was carrying the Messiah, God's Son."

He continued, "Eight days after my birthday on the day of my circumcision, my relatives were helping to choose a name for me. My mom insisted on the name John and they all argued. Finally they turned to my father who had not spoken a word all this time. He looked at them and he looked at me and he said, 'His name is John.' Everyone then knew that I was born for a specific purpose."

"How amazing that is. I have heard and studied of God in my youth but what you are telling me shows God in a much different way. So what is this 'great purpose'?"

"I will continue," he said. "I was raised as a normal child but my hunger for the scriptures was unfathomable. When I became a man, I felt it was time to go off on my own. My parents knew that the time would come and we said our tearful goodbyes. I had little possessions but a knife. I knew that that was all I would need. I was compelled to go to the desert. It was cold and God provided an old camel that had died. I skinned it and it gave me a warm coat. I was hungry and God provided locusts and honey."

"I imagine the first time you had one was not easy."

"When you are hungry you eat what God provides. Now I have grown to love the taste."

I scratched at my teeth and worked a locust leg out from between my teeth. John smiled, and then I begged him to continue his story.

He went on.

"God began to show me how all of mankind is wandering in a desert looking for something but they don't know what. They eat but are not filled and they drink but are never satisfied. People think that if only they had more money they can find what they are missing. That isn't how it works."

He stopped a moment closed his eyes then continued.

"The people are looking for a savior, the Messiah, to free them from Roman oppression and make them rich. That Messiah is in our midst, living among us today. I was sent to prepare the people for his coming."

"So you are telling people to take up swords and prepare for battle?"

He rolled his head back and laughed out loud.

"No, no! That is what most people thought would happen. That is why God needed me. The oppression men feel comes from within themselves. Getting rid of that oppression starts with repentance from your sins."

"That doesn't make sense. How can that be?"

"You are a Hebrew, right?"

I nodded and he continued.

"One of the first things you were taught in school was the Ten Commandments. They were simple and you probably thought they were easy to follow. All you had to do was love and honor God and family, and then the general living commandments: don't kill, don't lie, don't covet, don't steal and so forth. As we grow older, these commandments take a back seat to life and we go on disobeying them. That is, we sin."

As soon as he mentioned stealing something jolted inside of me. Everything I had stolen flashed before my eyes.

"Everyone has sinned. That is why I was born and that is my mission. I am here to call everybody to repent of their sins. Then when they have repented, I take them to the water and I baptize them as a sign of cleansing to show the world they have repented."

"Everyone has sinned," he repeated, "everyone except one."

"This is too hard to believe! No one can go through life without doing one wrong thing!"

"In ourselves we can't live a sin-free life, but remember I told you that the Messiah was God's son. He came to earth to show that it could be done. He also knows how hard it is. I have come to tell you to repent of your sins and He has come so your sins may be forgiven."

"You said this Messiah is living among us. Have you seen Him?"

"Yes, a while back I was baptizing people in the Jordan River and he was next in line. I knew immediately who he was. Here I was baptizing people as a sign of repentance of sins and he who had no sin came up to be baptized. I told him he should be baptizing me but he said that he needed 'to fulfill all righteousness.' Those were his exact words. He has a mission too just like I have a mission and everyone else. I then baptized him and immediately the Spirit in the form of a dove came on him. Then I heard a voice from heaven saying, 'this is my beloved Son in whom I am well pleased.' Then He left. I have not seen him since but I have heard stories of a man who goes about healing the sick. This could be him."

For the first time in my life, the guilt of all I had done weighed heavily on my heart. Maybe my father and grandfather would have still been alive. Maybe I wouldn't have had to be a slave. Oh, but then I wouldn't have met Marina. If I hadn't met Marina, then I wouldn't have this pain in my heart but maybe I would have met another girl. The questions and scenarios kept coming up.

John sat there quietly while all he said rolled over in my mind. Finally, I spoke and told him my whole life story. He listened patiently only nodding and giving me encouraging words. He neither judged me nor reprimanded me but listened with a kind ear. When I was finished, I sat waiting for him to speak.

"You have done nothing that cannot be repented of and you have done nothing that cannot be forgiven by the Messiah. Man, on the other hand, does not so easily forgive."

"What can I do?"

"Do not steal anymore. Make amends with those that you have stolen from. Love your enemies. Seek God with your whole heart."

As the fire was dying, we settled in for the night. I thought about all that John had said as I drifted off to sleep.

In the morning John left. He said that he had to

cross the river. I asked where I might find this Messiah.

"Just follow the crowds; if you seek him, you will find him." He continued with sadness, "I believe our future does not look easy but hold fast to the truth."

With that, he was gone.

CYNTHIA THILLET

MY NAME IS EZRA *(THE THIEF ON THE CROSS)*

DOWN BY THE SEA

I stayed at that camp pondering all that John had said. How could I make amends for my father's death? How could I repay all that I had stolen? How could I return a horse that was long gone? I had no answers. Worst of all was my great anger for Atticus. For six years I worked so hard for him and he denied me the love of my life, sweet Marina. Every time I thought of her I remembered her blue eyes, her silky black hair and the touch of her lips on mine. I would have stayed and worked with him forever if only Marina could have been mine.

Finally, I decided that I needed to see my mother so I headed north to the Sea of Galilee. I took my time, following the river. Sometimes game was plentiful and sometimes I had little to eat. These times I looked for locusts. Though I didn't have honey, they did give me some nourishment.

One night there was a fierce storm that lasted three days. I found a crag in the hill and hunkered down. The wind was so strong I could not even get a fire going. I ate what smoked meat I had and stayed there for the duration. I was thankful for my beard to warm my face but my clothes were of little help because the weather had made them nearly threadbare. My sandals were worn almost through; my hair was long and scruffy. I had become a man.

At dawn when the storm was finally over, I packed and headed up over the hill. There below me was the Sea of Galilee. There were fishing boats all around it and the morning sun was gleaming off it. I wanted to run down and jump in it. Instead, I looked the area over trying to guess where my family might be. There were a few small towns around the lake in which I was hoping there were no Roman soldiers.

I traveled along the lake enjoying the sun and the blue waters.

As I neared the village of Capernaum I could see

the smoke from the fires of people roasting their catch. There were people on the beach mending their nets and scores of boats on the lake. I wondered if one was Chalev's boat.

I took a quick swim to try and wash off some of the grime from the past week. When I came out, I gathered my things and went to see if I could warm up and dry off near one of the fires. As I neared one, a stranger by the fire called out.

"Shalom neighbor," he said. "You look hungry and we have had a good catch. Come join us."

"Thanks!" I replied. "I haven't had a good meal in three days. I got caught out in the storm for a few days and haven't had a chance to cook a meal."

They handed me a fish on a stick and between bites I asked them about their catch. They took me to the water's edge and showed me the fish flopping in the boat and some still in the nets.

"This looks like a great haul. Is fishing usually this good?"

"Lately it has been pretty good but a while back it was really bad. For days all we were catching was barely enough to keep us afloat. Then one morning after fishing all night long without catching a thing, we were about ready to give up fishing altogether.

"We had just pulled some nets out of the boat to clean them and had sat down when this large crowd comes over the hill following a man. They were crowding Him. Then this man climbs in a boat and with calm authority tells our friends to take him out on the lake a little way. I don't know why but they did. Maybe it was out of curiosity or just the tone of his voice. They paddled out where the water was about six feet deep and he sat in the boat and began to talk to the people on the shore. The crowd was large so we grabbed our nets and got in our boats also.

"He was telling the people to love their neighbors and show kindness whenever they could. He said their Father in heaven would see their good works and reward them. He told them to repay evil with good and forgive those who do wrong so they too can be forgiven. When he was done speaking he told our friends to row out on the lake a little more. We followed because the crowd was still out on the land. We heard him tell our friends to cast their nets in the water. They explained that they, like us, had been fishing all night and caught nothing. Then I heard our friend Peter say that just because he said to do it, he would. So as tired as they were they threw the nets once again into the water. Almost immediately the nets were so full they started to tear. They shouted for us to come and help. We had so much fish that it filled both boats.

"We rowed back to shore. Then this man looks at Peter and his brother and tells them to follow him and he will make them fishers of men. To our amazement, they left their boats in our charge and straight away followed him. Since then we have never had a really bad day fishing."

"Who was this man? Have you seen him since?"

"They call him Jesus of Nazareth. He had been preaching in the synagogues in the area. I have heard stories of him healing the sick, and causing the blind to see."

"Where is he now? How can I find Him?"

"He is not in one place long. He comes here from time to time, and he and his followers use the boat to cross the sea. I haven't seen Him lately."

"Do you know a fisherman by the name of Chalev?"

"Yes, do you see that boat out there? It is to the left the farthest one out. That is his boat. Do you know him?"

He is a friend of my family. Do you know where they live?"

He gave me directions to their house and I thanked them for their kindness.

Could this Jesus be the same man that John talked about? As I walked, I compared both stories in my mind. The man said that he healed the sick. I wondered if he could take away this anger and brokenness that I had inside. My desire to find this man grew.

MY NAME IS EZRA *(THE THIEF ON THE CROSS)*

MOM, ONCE MORE

I went into town and checked to see if there were Romans in the area. I saw none and people were going about their normal business so I guessed there were none.

I could see the house from quite a way off. There in the yard was my mother working on her mending. Two girls came out of the house and she kissed each one as she sent them on their way.

"Could that be Seleta and Ruth?" I wondered.

They looked much taller and seemed happy as they skipped in the opposite direction. I looked again at my mother. She was the same as I remembered except she had aged greatly, but she appeared to be content. Then I noticed a little boy playing at her feet. Was that my new brother? Things had changed for them but the changes looked good.

I stood watching them for a while enjoying the little scene before me. I almost walked away but I wanted to be near my mother and hug her and have her hug me back. I didn't know how much I missed her until that moment.

Slowly I walked toward her. She didn't notice me at first. Then she looked up. As I approached, she stood up suddenly and grabbed the baby and started to back slowly toward the house. I stopped.

I spoke. "Don't you know me? Don't you remember me? Mother, I am Ezra, your son."

She looked me up and down and then she looked into my eyes.

"It is you!"

Then she ran the rest of the way and gave me the biggest hug.

She hurried me into the house where she set out some bread and cheese. It had been so long since I had that, that it was like a feast to me. We talked a bit about the girls and baby Dan and how Chalev was doing with the fishing business. Then she asked about my life with Atticus. I told her all the work I had to do. Then when I told her about Marina she was not pleased.

"Ezra! Don't you know that Romans and Israelites don't mix? They are the enemy. They come into town and treat us like dogs."

"But Momma I loved her, and she loved me. Then when I asked Atticus permission for us to marry he forbade it. I would have stayed and worked forever if only I could have Marina's hand in marriage and he refused. After that, he was going to put me in a field to work like Grandfather did to keep me away from Marina, so I left. I could not stay any longer to work for that man."

"How did you get away without them catching you?"

"I stole a horse and rode for days. All I could think of was getting away."

"Oh my Goodness! You stole a horse and ran away? Don't you know what they do to runaway slaves? They have been crucifying them and leaving them to hang as an example. And you stole a horse? Oh! What will they do to you when they find you?"

"What is crucifying?"

"That is when they nail them to a tree and let them slowly die. It is horrible."

I was stunned. I knew I had done wrong, but I didn't think it was that bad. After my talk with John, I even thought of finding the horse and returning and asking forgiveness. Now I could never go back. Never could I make amends for what I had done. Now, what choices did I have? I was a criminal. Maybe I could stay with my mother. So I asked her.

"You can't stay here. A while back the Romans came and searched the whole house. They wouldn't say what they were looking for. They turned over everything. The house was in shambles. They kept asking 'where is he?' They kept threatening us. When they finally left, they said they would return. Now I know they were looking for you."

"Where am I supposed to go? What am I supposed to do?"

"I don't know. Let God lead you."

When she mentioned God, it reminded me of my conversation with John and what he said, "Confess your sins."

"I will leave then, but I must confess something to you. From a small boy, I have been a thief. It started off with just fruit and rolls, but I have taken more. Sometimes I would take money out of Dad's money pouch. One time Dad found out, and I ran out of the shop. I heard crashing sounds, but I kept running. Eventually, I ran home. I woke up to sounds of people crying and heard Dad was burned in a fire. Mother, Dad's death was my fault."

"When you came home early that night I knew something was not right. Then when you didn't cry at the burial, I guessed that you had something to do with it."

"So you knew?"

"I didn't want to know, but in my heart I did. I felt bad for you. I knew that you would have to live with this guilt and pain all your life. All sin has to be repaid some way. Maybe your time as a slave was meant to be a repayment for that. I don't know. I know that sending you to Atticus was the only possible solution to repay a debt our family owed. I wish it were not so. Do not let what you have done worry you any longer. We have a happy life now. You must go now before word gets out that you were here."

She packed me some bread and cheese and some smoked fish then found me a robe and sandals that belonged to Chalev and had me to change.

I gave her one last hug and said good-bye. I knew it would be the last time I saw her.

As I left, she said, "Maybe God still has a purpose for your life."

MY NAME IS EZRA *(THE THIEF ON THE CROSS)*

THE SERMON ON THE MOUNT

I left town heading north. Not far out of town there was a large crowd of people all going the same direction.

"Where are you headed?" I asked.

"We are following the Messiah!"

"The Messiah!"

"Yes! Jesus, the Messiah, have you not heard all the miracles he has been doing?"

"I have heard of some things."

"Well, he has healed the sick, made the blind to see and so much more. We want to see what he will do next."

"Where is He?"

"Up front surrounded by His disciples."

Is this the man John talked about? I had to see Him. I had to talk to Him. Maybe he would know what I could do.

As we climbed a hill I tried to push through the crowds to get a better look but everyone else was doing the same. At the top of the hill I could make out a man surrounded by a few others. Was that Him?

When he got to the top of the hill, he turned around and raised his hands and everybody sat. At this time I noticed soldiers on horseback mingling through the crowds. I caught a glimpse of one. It was Atticus. I could see that he was searching the crowd. I stayed low and listened as Jesus began to speak. I was so far away that I could not make out his face but I heard every word clearly. That voice I would never forget.

"Blessed are the poor in spirit: for theirs is the kingdom of heaven.

"Blessed are they that mourn: for they shall be

comforted.

"Blessed are the meek: for they shall inherit the earth.

"Blessed are they which do hunger and thirst after righteousness: for they shall be filled.

"Blessed are the merciful: for they shall obtain mercy.

"Blessed are the pure in heart: for they shall see God.

"Blessed are the peacemakers: for they shall be called the children of God.

"Blessed are they that are persecuted for righteousness' sake: for theirs is the kingdom of heaven.

"Blessed are you when men shall revile you, and persecute you, and shall say all manner of evil against you falsely, for my sake.

"Rejoice, and be exceedingly glad: for great is your reward in heaven: for so persecuted they the prophets which were before you."

The soldiers were circling now toward the back of the crowd. I had to get away. Every time Atticus turned his back I scooted farther back. When he turned around, I froze. When I got out of the crowd, I lay flat on the grass until he turned away then made my way to the tall thicket.

I could not make out all his words now but as the wind blew, I caught parts. I moved not a muscle as I tried to hear what he said.

"But I say unto you, love your enemies, bless them that curse you, do good to them that hate you, and pray for those who despitefully use you, and persecute you."

Did that mean Atticus? Did he mean to love Atticus?

"Therefore I say unto you, take no thought for your life, what you shall eat, or what you shall drink; nor yet for your body, what you shall put on. Is not life more than food, and the body more than clothing?"

I always had food to eat even in the wild. Even when my water supply was low, the rains came. And when my clothes were in tatters my mother gave me a new set. Could this have been God?

"Lay not up for yourselves treasures upon earth, where moth and rust corrupt, and where thieves break through and steal: but lay up for yourselves treasures in heaven, where neither moth nor rust corrupts, and where thieves do not break through nor steal:

For where your treasure is, there will your heart be also."

When I heard him speak the word "thief" it went right through me.

I sat huddled in the thicket afraid to move until the last person dispersed. The last to leave were the Roman guard and they passed within a stone's throw of me.

As they passed, I heard Atticus say, "Let us go back to his mother's house to see if he has been there."

In my mind, Jesus' words kept repeating over and over. It sounded like he was talking about my mother. How blessed she must be. I said a prayer for her safety as I dared to breathe.

I waited till dark to leave my location. I wanted to follow the crowds to see where this Jesus went next but I didn't know which way they went and I knew I had to stay away from crowds as much as possible.

MY NAME IS EZRA *(THE THIEF ON THE CROSS)*

THE WOMAN AT THE WELL

I headed back towards the west. I didn't keep track of where I went or how long I stayed. I ate what I could find and slept when I was tired. I wandered probably for a few months without talking to anyone. If I heard anyone coming, I hid in the brush and let them pass until they were well out of hearing range.

Once when I needed water, I came across a large well. I could hear the water in the bottom of the well but I had nothing to draw it up. I sat there in the shade a while hoping someone would come. After an hour a woman approached. She was older than me but not yet my mother's age and very attractive. She looked at me and proceeded to draw water for herself.

When she was finished I asked her if she might

draw me some also. She looked at me as if she could see through me and then spoke.

"I will draw you water but if you had the water I know about you will never thirst again."

"There is no such water as that," I said.

"That is what I once thought until I learned about the living water."

At that moment I had never felt thirstier. "Show me this water," I begged.

"Where is your home?" she asked.

"I have no home. My father is dead, and I cannot return to my mother's house. I fled from the last place I lived. Even now they are searching for me."

Why I said all that I knew not. I didn't know who the woman was, but for some reason, I felt I could trust her.

"You speak the truth. Come with me. You look worn out and I will feed you and tell you of this 'living water.'"

I followed like a small child not knowing where she would lead me. I offered to carry her jug of water but she refused. We walked in silence.

She led me to a small house with a bench outside under a small shade tree. She told me to sit while she went inside.

When she came out she had a tray of bread, cheese and fruit. It looked like a feast to me. I wanted to gobble it down as fast as I could but remembering that I was in the presence of a real lady and there was a story to be heard, so I took my time.

"Tell me of this 'living water.'"

"When you are thirsty there is nothing that can satisfy you more than water. When your soul is thirsty there is nothing that can satisfy you except living water. Everyone is searching to fill a void in their life. They try and fill it with possessions, money or even love, but none of that can really satisfy that thirst that is deep within us. That can only come from knowing God."

"I have known about God since I was a young lad. My father told me stories about Him."

"Many people know God that way and go about their ways like He is somewhere far off. God is not like that. He wants us to be his friend. He loves us so much and cares about us even more. All He asks us in return is for us to love Him back and to show his love to others. When we are consumed by his love, joy flows out of us and nothing can take that joy away. When we live in that joy, the problems that come our way seem small. We know that because God loves us whatever comes our way will be all right."

"How do you know all this?"

"Some time ago I was drawing water from that same well and a man was sitting right where you were. He asked me for a drink and then told me of my life without even knowing me. Just think, I am a Samaritan and he was a Jew. Then he told me of this 'living water.' He said we must worship God in Spirit and in truth. I told him that I heard that the Messiah was coming and he would explain all things. Then he told me *he* was the Messiah! I dropped my water jug and ran to town and told everyone to come and meet the Messiah.

I went back to the well and a whole crowd of

people was following me. They all wanted to meet this man, the Messiah. He and his disciples ended up staying in our village for three days teaching us."

"How do I get this living water?"

"Believe that he is the Messiah, the Son of God, the One coming to save us. When we do that, we acknowledge his love for us, and then he will grant us eternal life. Just imagine!"

"Where do I find this Messiah? What is his name?"

"His name is Jesus. I don't know where to find Him. He goes to Jerusalem for the Passover every year. That is not too far off."

"I need to find Him."

I thanked her for the food and headed on my way.

CYNTHIA THILLET

MY NAME IS EZRA *(THE THIEF ON THE CROSS)*

THE SEARCH

Again I was wandering the countryside. I had no destination and no plans. As I wandered I kept thinking about this Messiah, this Jesus. Who was He? I needed to find Him. Maybe he had answers for me.

What was to become of me? I was still young. What purpose was there to my life? Was I to wander for the rest of my life hiding from people? At one time I could picture my life with a wife and children. Now what hope was there for me?

At night I would sleep fitfully, dreaming of my father and the crash I heard before the fire that killed him. Often I would wake up screaming. In another dream, I would see these treasures before my eyes. I would reach out and take one. As soon as my hand touched one, it would become a venomous snake. Another dream I had was when I was riding that beautiful horse. I felt so free and happy. Then all of a sudden a thorny hedge would be before me. I tried to escape the hedge but the more I tried to ride out of it the thicker it got. I would wake up flailing my arms in the air trying to break out of this hedge.

During the day it was a fight for survival. I had to fight to get food. I had to find shelter from the storms and cold. Other times wild animals would smell my food and I would have to fight them off. My sling was always close at hand. I became so attuned to the sounds that I could hear the footsteps of animals and knew which ones were friendly, which ones were food and which ones wanted me for food.

The more I thought about Jesus, the more I knew that peace for me would only come through finding this man and getting this living water.

At times I would walk on the main roads hoping I would run into someone that knew of him and could tell me where he was. I would hear of healings he did but nobody seemed to know where he was.

One really hot day I saw a big shade tree in the distance. It was like an oasis to me and I headed for it. A man was sitting under it so I asked if he would mind if I sat also. There was nothing special about Him. He carried no pack yet he did not look hungry.

I set my pack down a proper distance away, stretched out and watched the man. He seemed to be totally at peace with his surroundings.

He looked at me and I felt like he could see right through me. Finally he spoke.

"You look very tired. Are you thirsty? I have water."

"No," I replied, "I have water."

I took a long drink of my water. I didn't want to drink his since it seemed that he only had a small pouch.

"Do you live around here?" I asked.

"No," he said. "I am only traveling through. One day soon I will return to My Father's house. Until then I must finish the work my Father has for me to do here. Where My Father lives very few have been but one day many will be allowed to go. It is paradise and I miss it."

"Why don't you go to your Father's home now?"

"If I go now then no one will ever be allowed to go there with me."

His words were very confusing to me, so I remained silent.

"Where are you headed?" he asked.

"I am going to Jerusalem to find a man. I heard that he was going to be there for the Passover and I have business with Him."

I got up to leave.

"Are you sure you don't need anything?" he asked.

"I don't believe you have anything I need," I said.

"I pray you find everything you are looking for."

With that, I headed on my way to find the Messiah.

MY NAME IS EZRA *(THE THIEF ON THE CROSS)*

QUESTIONS

As I walked I thought of that stranger. His voice reminded me of one I heard before but I couldn't place it. Where was his kingdom? What kind of work prevented him from going home?

All that night I thought of these questions. In the morning, I rethought the whole conversation and more came to my remembrance. He offered me water just like the woman at the well said the Messiah did. Could that have been the Messiah? That *voice*! It was the one I heard on the mountain when Jesus spoke. It was the Messiah!

Why didn't I recognize him? Maybe because he wasn't surrounded by a crowd as people said he would be? Maybe because there was nothing in his appearance that would make him seem important? Or maybe I was too focused on finding him when he was right before my eyes.

Whatever it was I had to go back to see if I could find him. Maybe I would catch him on this road to Jerusalem. I passed several groups of people but he was not a part of any of them. Maybe he was still in the area of the tree. I reached the tree late at night and no one was there. I decided to camp under the tree that night to see if anyone showed up the next day. All day I sat and waited and though a few came to cool off in the shade I didn't recognize any of them.

I wish I had that time that I spent with him under the tree back again. I wanted that peace that he had. I had so many questions to ask Him.

I was tired of roaming the wilderness without purpose to my life. I had no friends. I couldn't see my family. What was I to do? What would become of my life?

If he were the Son of God as John had said, then surely he would know what I could do to make my life better, to give my life purpose.

I had to find Him. All I knew was that he went to Jerusalem every year for the Passover, so I went with my original plan and headed back on the way to Jerusalem.

I hadn't eaten for several days since I was in a hurry to get back to the tree, so I camped in a grassy area near a pond. The rabbits and fish were plentiful so I stayed a few days. I tried to relax and enjoy my time there and not think of what my life had become. My dreams at night, however, did not give me the peace I needed.

I stayed at the camp drying out meat for my travel to Jerusalem. Little did I know that this was the last meat I would ever have.

CYNTHIA THILLET

MY NAME IS EZRA *(THE THIEF ON THE CROSS)*

ENTRY INTO JERUSALEM

Passover was just over a week away, so I had to hurry to get to the city. I decided to take the main roads for a more direct route. They were crowded with groups of families all trying to get to Jerusalem. It was easier to fall in behind one of these groups to avoid detection from the Romans patrolling the roads.

When it got late a large group camped alongside the road and I also stayed on the outskirts of the camp. I got a small fire going, ate my dried meat and settled in for the night. I didn't sleep well. I had never been to Jerusalem but I had heard stories about it. I knew there would be many Roman Soldiers there and that scared me. Even so, I knew I had to find Messiah Jesus if ever I was going to have peace in my life. Somehow deep inside me, I knew that this was the only way. So, soldiers or not I had to go.

The next day we started out early. By noon we had come to the top of a small mountain. There below in all its glory was the city. The walls of the city were huge. You could see people as small as ants going in and out of the massive gates. My heart was racing. I never saw such a majestic site. I wanted to run the rest of the way but I knew that would be certain capture for me.

I stayed tight with the group I was following. Progress was slow that last mile. More people started joining us as we traveled. Finally we made it to the gate. There were guards, tax collectors, and merchants everywhere. I kept my head low and followed the family in front of me. Their excitement made them oblivious to my presence. Once through the gate, I separated myself and hid in the shadows on a side road.

I needed a plan. How was I going to find this Messiah and where was I going to stay until I did. First, I decided that the temple would be the best place to look for Jesus since he often taught in the synagogues. I made my way there taking side streets keeping an eye out for where a person could sleep for the night. I found a few boarding places but my money had been spent long ago. It would have been easy for me to obtain more, for I saw lots of men's pouches just hanging in the open on their belt. One swipe of my knife and I would have had plenty. With all the guards around, though, I didn't want to take the chance.

When I made it to the temple, it was not as I had expected. I expected a quiet place of worship and sacrifice. What I saw was worse than the marketplace with people hollering trying to get the out-of-towners to come to their table to get the best sacrifice. I noticed some of the doves they were selling had been coated to cover their flaws. Still, they were selling them for perfect specimens. The merchant was talking so fast that the buyers were too confused and flustered to get a good look at the birds before they had their money turned over.

When they turned their birds in for a sacrifice they were often told that it wasn't enough and had to pay an exorbitant amount of money also. They were left almost penniless.

When they finally got a chance to go in and worship they were hurried and shoved out of the way to make room for more people. Even though this place was huge they were fighting over positions for the best place to worship.

Many were praying in such loud voices saying how repentant they were and thanking God they made such a large offering. One that I noticed had ended up penniless and was huddled in a small corner crying because she wished she could have done more.

In some areas, a Rabbi would be teaching a small group of people. This is where I expected to find Jesus but he was nowhere to be found. I left feeling dejected.

It was late and I was tired and hungry. I needed a place to sleep, but there was nowhere outside the gates, and stopping to rest would be taking a chance because many soldiers were patrolling the area. I decided to head toward the marketplace to see if I could possibly find something to eat. There was a large crowd all trying to find something for their evening meal. I was being pushed and shoved in every direction.

There was a man so close in front of me that had a moneybag dangling from his belt. Without thinking, I pulled out my knife, cut the cord and grabbed the pouch. Then I quickly pushed back through the crowd before anyone knew what happened. I went to another part of the market and found a bread stand where I purchased a small loaf of bread and some cheese. That left just enough money to have a place to sleep.

I went and hid in the shadows of a building and quickly ate the bread. Every bite stuck in my mouth. I had to force it down. A gloom came over me. As I heard the words that John had spoken to me, "Do not steal," I tried to reason with myself that I was hungry and tired and needed food but that was little comfort.

Now that I was no longer hungry I went back to a boarding place. They looked at me suspiciously but took my money and showed me to a cot in a dark and dingy room. I slept fitfully that night overcome by guilt.

I woke the next morning still determined to find Jesus. I walked aimlessly through the streets feeling like there was no hope for me. I looked through the temple and did not see Jesus. My heart was heavy my stomach still felt the bread that was now like lead in me. I didn't think that Jesus could help me anymore. At the gate, I heard people shouting, "Jesus is coming!"

I ran out the gate and saw coming down the hill a large crowd of people lining the road. Many had branches in their hand, waving them in the air and shouting. At the front of the procession was a man riding on a donkey. People were throwing their coats on the ground in front of Him. As they came closer I could recognize the man. It was Jesus. At last I would get a chance to talk to him. The crowd grew larger forming a path to the gate. I could make out what they were shouting.

"Hosanna to our King! Blessed is he who comes in the name of the Lord for he has done great things. Hosanna! Blessed is the coming Kingdom of David!"

The shouting got louder as they reached the gate. I tried to get close to see Jesus but the crowds were too thick. The more I pushed forward, the more people came and pushed me back. How was I ever to get to talk to him with all these people surrounding Him? Then he was even with me. I tried to stay up with him but couldn't. Just when I was ready to turn in despair, he looked directly at me. He saw through me. He saw my desperation. He saw my hurt. Yet, I could feel his love radiate through me.

"Hosanna to the living God!" I shouted with tears in my eyes.

I stayed with the crowd shouting along with them. When I finally did get to the front, Jesus had disappeared. I wanted to follow him and be part of his group. I wanted to learn more. I knew that he was the Messiah and had what I had been searching for. But where was He?

I turned back toward the gate. It was getting late but the streets were still packed with people. There were soldiers on horseback everywhere but the crowd was large so I didn't worry. As I walked I passed a merchant selling fruit. In front, there was a mound of apples stacked high. They were shiny and the deepest red. At that moment one apple fell off the table onto the ground. I picked it up and remembered the first time I had tasted one. I pictured the sweet juiciness of it as I had taken my first bite. Then I remembered my dream. All of a sudden I heard a voice holler.

"Thief!"

I turned around and saw no one that was stealing

or running. Then I saw soldiers coming toward me. I still had the apple in my hand. I looked at the merchant and he was shouting at me. I hurriedly put the apple back but it was too late. The soldiers were dismounting their horses and coming toward me. To my horror, one was Atticus.

"Finally we have found you, you thief. You shall pay for what you did."

I tried to run but the crowd blocked my way. Within minutes they had me on the ground tying ropes around my wrists. I tried to struggle but they were too strong. They dragged me to my feet and tied the other end of the rope to one of the horses. They snatched up my pack and tossed it over the other horse. Then they mounted their horses and started off. I stumbled behind them over the rocks in the road trying to keep up with them. At one point I fell to the ground and scraped my knees. I had to scramble back up to my feet while I was being dragged. The riders never looked back at me.

The crowd along the way was watching in disgust wondering what horrendous crime I had done. Many had smiles on their faces thinking that I had finally got caught. Some even threw stones and spit at me. Mothers shielded their children's eyes from me. I guess they thought whatever I had done would rub off on their little ones. I tried to keep my eyes down but navigating the rocks made it difficult.

By the time we made it to the palace away from the crowds, the rope had dug into my wrists and my knees were throbbing.

CYNTHIA THILLET

MY NAME IS EZRA *(THE THIEF ON THE CROSS)*

IMPRISONED

Atticus and the other rider turned me over to the guards at Herod's palace speaking a few words privately of my crimes. They untied my ropes and shackled my feet. Then the guards pushed me down a long hallway and two flights of steps. We were now underground as the windows were very high on the walls. The place was dank and quite dark and smelled awful. Ahead of me was a corridor with doors with bars on them. I could hear groaning and shouts coming from behind the doors as I got shoved along.

Finally, the guards stopped me and one guard opened one of the iron-barred doors while the other blocked my way of escape. Then he pushed me into the cell and the first guard took a chain that was attached to the wall and attached it onto my shackles. Their job was done. They turned back to the door and closed it with a heavy thud and I could hear the lock click into place. They went laughing down the hall.

It was almost completely dark. Only a dim light from the barred doors added any light. The smell was horrendous. Besides the smell of human waste there was the smell of rotting flesh. I could see shadows of other prisoners and hear their chains rattling but there was no idle chat. These prisoners seemed more dead than alive.

Was this to be my fate? Was I going to be left to slowly rot away while they decided what to do with me?

I took off my cloak and lay on the hard floor to try and sleep. I wondered what my mom would think if she knew where I was. I hoped that she would never find out. I thought of my life and wondered if I really deserved this punishment for what I did. I was angry and I was bitter. I wasn't going to steal that apple. But then I thought again of all the other things I did steal. Yes, I was a thief. I couldn't deny that. Some way they were going to make me pay for all I had done.

It wasn't Atticus' fault that he was right near me when I held that apple. He had lost a good worker who still owed him over a year's wages. He had lost a horse that was probably the most promising horse.

As I was about to fall asleep, I again saw the face of Jesus, and he was passing by me. That look of love calmed me now as I drifted off into an uncomfortable sleep.

CYNTHIA THILLET

MY NAME IS EZRA *(THE THIEF ON THE CROSS)*

FIRST TRIAL

I was awakened in the morning by a noise near the door. A pan of water was slid in through a slot in the door and some old bread was thrown in. None of the other prisoners stirred, so I scooped some water up with my hands and grabbed some bread. It was hard and had bits of mold on it but I hadn't eaten in two days so I picked off what mold parts I could see in the dimness and ate the rest. The other prisoners noticing the bread crawled over, one by one, lapped up some water, grabbed a piece of bread and went back to their places

I looked around to find a place to relieve myself but the only place I saw that I could reach was a corner of the cell. It appeared to have been used before so I also used it. The urine drained toward the center of the room where it emptied into a few cracks it found.

I went back to my wall and sat and waited for

what I knew not.

What seemed like a few hours later, I heard the door being unlocked. I must have dozed off because the noise startled me. One guard entered the cell and came toward me. He unlocked my shackles from the wall and ordered me to stand. I had trouble since I had been sitting a long time and my knees were still in pain. The guard showed no mercy as he shoved me toward the door. My hands were bound and they led me back the way I had entered. After a long walk and a flight of stairs we were above ground. I could see that it was very richly furnished in red drapes with gold fixtures.

I was led into a large room even more opulently decorated in which at least fifty men were seated as if they were at a banquet. They led me to the center of this group of men.

Finally, the man who looked like he was the leader spoke.

"Why do you bring this man to me on this Passover week? What crime has he done?"

A gentleman to my right moved forward. Up to

this point, I had not noticed him, and on further inspection, I realized that I had never met him before.

"He is a thief. We caught him in the marketplace stealing from our stands."

"And you thought that you should interrupt my time for a petty thief?" barked the leader.

"We cannot allow this thieving to continue. If every thief were let go we would lose all our profit and the thieves would run rampant in our town."

The leader looked to the other men in the room.

"What say you to this man's crimes?"

"Banishment!" "Ten floggings!" "Set him free, this man just wants blood!" They all called out something different.

The leader quieted the crowd.

"I do not want this matter to ruin a night's sleep, I sentence him to five floggings and then he shall be free."

I heard murmuring to my right and then this unknown man spoke again.

"Only five lashes? This man has stolen a Roman horse. Five floggings are not nearly enough."

"I said five. The prisoner is a Jew. I rule for what happens to Jews. If you want him tried for what happens to a Roman taken him to Pontius Pilate."

They took me out to a large courtyard where there were several posts. At one I could see one of the men from my cell being whipped. There was a large crowd outside the courtyard cheering each time one of the whips landed.

I heard them counting as the whip lashed through the air.

"Nine!" and then cheers.

"Ten!" and then they untied the man and he slumped to the ground.

The guards dragged the man to the gate, opened it and set the man outside and left him.

They looked at my captors and me, and signaled for them to bring me to them. I tried to pull back but knew it was no use. I didn't want what happened to that man to happen to me.

They lead me to a vacant post that had a large ring on top. It had blood running down it and pooled around the bottom. It was so low that when they bound my hands to the ring I was forced to my knees. The guards removed my cloak and stepped back.

I saw a huge man approaching wearing a leather mask to hide his features. In his hand was a whip. It was about eight feet long. The end of the whip split into smaller leather straps. At each end of the straps was secured a piece of sharp bone. I shuddered and shouted and again tried to shrink back away from the inevitable punishment that was coming my way.

The masked man looked at the guards and asked, "How many?"

"Five," they sneered. Then they moved back.

The punisher waved his whip over his head much like I did with my sling. It whirred loudly and then came down fast and hard on my back.

I screamed as one of the bones dug into my cheek.

"One!" the crowd hollered. I saw the first apple I had stolen and the coins gleaming in my hand.

Again the masked man swung his whip. This time I braced for the impact hiding my face in my arms.

"Two!" I saw my sling burning in my hand.

"Three!" I saw the knife and remembered the beating I should have got from stealing the money from my dad.

I deserved this I thought and I cried for the loss of my dad that I had caused. This was the first time I had allowed myself to cry for my father. The pain of losing my dad hurt far worse than the beating I received. For the first time I was genuinely sorry for what I had done.

"Four!" The bones tore into my skin as I remembered the fragrance I stole to attract Marina. She was beautiful but she was young and naive, and so was I. Was she really the one for me? I doubted it now.

The whip was whirling in the air now a very long time and I looked up to see the abuser smiling and looking into the crowd as he geared up to give the final blow. I braced myself.

"Five!"

The crowd cheered as the punisher finished his job and stepped back.

Blood was dripping steadily down my back to the front of me as I pictured the moneybag. Did I really need it or had stealing just been a part of me so long. I deserved this beating I had received. I felt totally abandoned, useless and broken.

Then I remembered the last time I saw Jesus. He looked at me as though he knew everything I had done. That look was not the look that my guards gave me or the one the crowds gave me or even the look of pity my mother gave me. He loved me unconditionally and I knew it. What could this love do for me now? I didn't know but as I collapsed in a heap I felt at peace.

I felt hands pull me up. I could barely stand. How could anyone endure more flogs than I had received? My back was in indescribable pain as they threw my cloak over my shoulders. Instead of releasing me outside the gate, they took me back to the dark cell and laughed as they said, "Now we shall see what Pilate thinks of this thief."

I was alone now in the cell. Slowly I peeled off my cloak loosening it from the partly dried blood covering my emaciated back. I tried to hold my groans in but the pain of my skin ripping as I tugged off the cloak was too great. There was some water left in the bowl from the early meal, so I took a long drink and washed the cut on my cheek. Then I slowly poured the water down my back to rinse some of the blood away. I covered the front of me with my cloak leaving my back in the open and though it was quite early I slept.

I woke up when I heard a noise at the door and saw water and bread pushed through. I drank some water, poured the rest down my back, then fell asleep.

All the next day I dozed on and off. I woke for a short time when the guards brought in a new man or when they pushed food in. When I had to relieve myself and I stood up the sores in my back cracked open and started bleeding again.

MY NAME IS EZRA *(THE THIEF ON THE CROSS)*

SECOND TRIAL

The following morning when the door opened two Roman guards stood there in full uniform.

"Ezra!" They called.

I jumped tearing open some sores. They came to me, unfastened my fetters from the wall and jerked me to my feet. I put my cloak on and they walked me out with my hands tied behind my back.

They walked me to a large open veranda where more soldiers gathered. Atticus was in the group.

After a few minutes the doors to my left opened and out walked a very tall thin man with a crown of leaves on his head. All in the area immediately came to attention. I figured this must be Pontius Pilate.

Pilate looked at me and then at my accusers.

"What charges have you brought against this man?" he asked in a high irritating voice.

"We would not have brought him to you if his crimes were not very grave. This man was a slave of your faithful soldier Atticus when he stole a large amount of gold and a valuable horse and ran away."

Pilate looked at Atticus.

"Is this true?"

Atticus clicked his heels together and answered, "Yes Sir!"

"How long did he have to serve?"

"He had just over a year to serve," Atticus replied.

Pilate looked at me and then back at Atticus.

"He was one of our trusted slaves. We even shared a table with him."

Pilate looked at me and questioned, "Why did you run away? Were you beaten?"

"No," I replied.

"Were you starving?"

"No."

"Were you doing work that was too hard?"

"No."

I didn't know then that life as a slave could have been so much worse for me. I only had one more year and I would have been free with money to start a life of my own, yet I chose to run.

"Then why did you run away?"

How could I tell the truth? How foolish it all sounded now.

"I could no longer live in a place where my love was and not be allowed to be around her."

With that everyone in the area burst into a hearty laugh.

"Silence!" Pilate bellowed.

Immediate silence followed.

"So you then stole the most valued horse and gold

and ran?"

"Yes."

"Where is this horse now?"

"I don't know. It was stolen from me."

To the group Pilate asked, "What has become of this horse that was supposed to win the chariot race for us?"

An unknown soldier replied, "It has become dinner for a band of murderers."

"What!!!!!!"

I knew then that I would not have any sympathy from Pilate.

He looked at me and asked, "What have you to say for yourself now?"

"I will work twenty years to pay for what I have done."

"Do you think that twenty years will bring back a horse that took years to find? What man would want you to work for him after you have run away? You are useless to anybody."

He paced around the room then asked the gathered men. "What shall we do with this thief and runaway slave?"

"Crucify him!" they shouted. "Let him be an example for all other slaves that run away. We do not want this problem to continue."

"Yes that is the only way," Pilate answered satisfied. "And put a sign above him that all who see him will know what he has done. Now get him out of here."

"NO!!!" I shouted, falling to my knees.

They led me out forcefully.

Crucify me? Was this what was to become of me? Was my life to end so soon and so horribly? How much time before this thing happened to me?

CYNTHIA THILLET

MY NAME IS EZRA *(THE THIEF ON THE CROSS)*

ANOTHER CELL

They took me to a different cell in the dark, dreary hall.

Again they shackled my feet to the wall.

"Enjoy what little time you have left along with these ruffians."

Two other men were already in there.

I recognized one immediately.

Gestes the very guy that stole my horse was in one corner. He glared at me when he saw me. The other man was a big burly man.

I was chained in one of the vacant corners far enough from the other men where they couldn't reach me, nor I them.

As soon as the door shut Gestes confronted me.

"You told me that horse was your horse. If I had known it was a Roman horse I wouldn't have stolen it. Then they wouldn't be getting ready to hang me."

"If you didn't steal it maybe neither of us would have been here. But I believe that the horse made no difference to the Romans in deciding our fate. They wanted an example and we are sitting here waiting to die."

"It was the horse that got me caught."

"How is that?" I asked.

I knew the answer but I wanted to hear it from him.

"Well, the horse was getting lame and we were getting hungry. So we skinned him and smoked him and ate well off of him. But I guess that the Romans saw the horse's skinning and followed our trail."

"Bwahaha!" laughed the other guy. "What fools you were. You deserve to be here if you were that careless to leave a trail that big. But horse-eating definitely isn't a reason to get you in this place."

"It might not have been unless it was a Roman chariot horse and for the fact that the Roman army is now short two of their finest."

Again the other man laughed.

"Well, at least I have fewer Romans to deal with when I get out of here."

"When you get out of here? I thought this was the place where they put those that will be crucified," I said.

"That may be what they think is going to happen to me but I know, somehow I know, that my fate will be different. And when I get out I will rid this country of this Roman tyranny that has overtaken it."

"Yeah, that will be the day. They let the likes of you out of here," guffawed Gestes.

At that time the door opened and pans of food were shoved in. This time it was a bit more substantial. I guessed that they wanted to keep us alive longer, so they fed us better. I was quite hungry so I ate every morsel.

I laid down to rest using my cloak again for a blanket but when I pulled it off my back the wounds on my back opened and despite myself I let out a holler. The other men looked at me and saw my back.

"That doesn't look good," one said but I was in too much pain to care. I tried to sleep as the others chatted away each bragging about the exploits they had done. Rest finally came.

We were awakened the next morning when Roman soldiers in their full regalia opened the door.

"Barabbas!" they shouted. "Get up! You are coming with us."

Barabbas, who seconds ago was snoring loudly, stirred and sat up.

As the soldier released him from the wall Barabbas questioned them.

"What is this all about? Where are you taking me?"

"This could be your lucky day," one answered. "They are choosing which prisoner is to be set free. They told us to grab the prisoner with the worst crimes against him. We chose you."

They led him out and locked the door behind them.

"Do you think he will be back?" I asked Gestes.

"With all he has done I would not be surprised if he were back very soon," he replied.

The door opened a short time later and we expected to see Barabbas return but it was only our breakfast.

"Eat up," the guard said, "this is your last meal."

We looked at our breakfast and there was fruit and bread.

We looked at the feast with wide eyes. We both knew but did not say what we were thinking. They wanted us to have strength so we would last longer for what was to befall us. Even so we ate with gusto.

Time passed and we saw no sign of Barabbas' return.

"Maybe he was right. Maybe he did get set free," said Gestes.

"If he did, who would have taken his place?" I wondered.

MY NAME IS EZRA *(THE THIEF ON THE CROSS)*

CARRYING THE CROSS

Around midday our door was opened again. This time it looked like a whole squadron of soldiers. They first take Gestes and lead him away. He tries to fight off the guard but is rewarded with a blow to his back. Then they come to me. I comply, as a blow to my back would open up more of the sores that are already festering.

Where was I going? Would it be over soon? I had no idea. I didn't know that in less than ten hours I would be dead.

They led us to the courtyard where I was flogged. Lying on the ground were three long logs about six feet long. Each log has a notch cut out at the center.

They turned toward Gestes' group and led him to one of the crossbeams lying down. It took two men to lift it. They removed Gestes' cloak and lifted the crossbeam to his back. Then another man tied his arms in place one on each side of the cross beam. His knees nearly buckled as he got the full weight of the crossbeam on his back.

When they were finished with him they turned to my group and started the whole process again. They took my cloak and left me only in my undergarment. I could hear the crossbeam behind me being lifted to where I was standing. They pulled one of my arms back and tied my arm to the crossbeam giving me just a slight bit of room to adjust. Then they grabbed my other arm and tied it to the other side. The guards holding the wood stepped back and the weight fell hard on my broken back. I could feel fresh blood oozing out of the reopened sores. My knees buckled with the pain and the weight. I fell to my knees and received a lash as they hollered at me to get up. Fortunately, the cross took most of the beating. I managed to stand. If I stayed very still, the wood from the cross didn't dig into my sores.

When they finished with me they led out the third victim. I was half expecting to see Barabbas but even though this Man's face was covered in blood and totally unrecognizable, he didn't have the bulk of Barabbas. For some reason they left his cloak on but you could see that it was fully covered in blood. He had some kind of thorny head covering that looked like a crown. They tied him to the cross the same way. I don't know how he managed the weight of the beam but he never stumbled.

Someone shouted for the gates to open. We were herded out the gates with soldiers flanking both sides of us. We headed out down a narrow road. Crowds started gathering along our way. The city was packed with people coming to celebrate Passover and it seemed like all of them were lining the roads as we made our way.

The unknown man was in the lead and he seemed to garner the most attention. I couldn't hear what the crowd was shouting to him over the loudness but many wanted to get near to him and touch him. The guards kept pushing them off so we could keep progressing.

As I passed, people were throwing rocks and cheering. I kept my head down. I was so weak now from all the blood loss that it took every ounce of my being to keep from falling and having my heavy load come crashing down on me. I knew I deserved this punishment.

I had let so many people down. I prayed that none of those people were along the road watching me. The shame of all that I had done was heavier than the weight I was carrying.

As we were going on an especially rocky part of the road, we came to a halt. The crowd got quiet and gasped. I could hear a guard shout, "You help him carry the cross." I guess the man in front could no longer carry his burden alone.

We proceeded out of the gates of the city. The crowd followed us and increased in size as the space around us widened. The guards, tired of being hit by rocks, kept the people farther away but they still hurled insults and vulgarities.

My weight felt increasingly heavy as we traveled up a rocky hill. I stumbled and fell. Immediately I was bludgeoned and forced to stand. I went slower to try and keep my footing more secure.

Finally we made it to the top of the hill where we stopped. I looked up and saw three immense poles lying on the ground about fifteen feet long. Their tops were resting on a mound of dirt. Near the top of each pole was cut a notch like the one on the beam I was carrying. At the foot of each was a deep hole.

They guided each of us to a separate pole. I was on the right, Gestes was on the left and the other man was in the middle. Three soldiers stayed with me and made me lie down next to the pole. I collapsed totally exhausted. If I were free I couldn't have run away if I tried. Each soldier grabbed an arm of the cross beam and the other grabbed my feet. Then they positioned the notch of the crossbeam over that of the pole. I was now lying at a slight angle as they secured the two pieces of wood together.

They walk away. Their part of the task is done.

CYNTHIA THILLET

MY NAME IS EZRA *(THE THIEF ON THE CROSS)*

BACK TO THE PRESENT

Once the pain settles down to a tolerable level, I look out over the immense crowd that has gathered. Some are crying, some are just curiosity seekers but a good portion is throwing insults. The soldiers are particularly interested in the one in the middle, this King of the Jews.

"Wait a minute," I think. "That sign said his name is Jesus. Is this the same man that I have been wanting to talk to? They said he was the Son of God. He shouldn't be here. He could call armies to rescue Him. I don't understand."

A few of the soldiers below are fighting over Jesus' robe. At first they wanted to tear it and share the pieces. Then one suggested they throw dice for it. They did. The winner holds it up over his head then suddenly drops it like it is on fire. When he picks it up it is with tenderness.

Jesus looks at the soldiers and speaks, *"Father, forgive them for they know not what they do."*

The soldiers below Jesus are mocking him now.

"Hey, King, why don't you save yourself?" one says.

"Yeah, you saved others, why don't you save yourself."

"You said you were going to build the temple in three days, how are you going to do that now?"

"Where are all your subjects now, great king?"

Gestes looks toward him and joins the mockery.

I am confused and join in also. "If you are the king why don't you save yourself?" Each word coming out of my mouth was a huge effort. I had to push up with my feet just to be able to get enough air.

"My God why hast thou forsaken me?" Jesus cries out.

"Even God has turned his back on the great king!" one guard shouts.

The soldiers back off from the cross and a small group of people walks up to the cross of Jesus. Among them are two ladies and a young man. They are all crying.

Jesus speaks to them.

"Mother, behold your son. Son, behold your mother." His voice is weak but even now I see how much he cares for his mother.

I wonder what my mother is doing. I hope she is not in this crowd. She has a new life and a new family. I wish I had done things differently so that I could be there for her and give her grandchildren.

Jesus speaks again, *"I thirst."*

A soldier steps up and dips a sponge on a long stick in some liquid. He puts it to his lips but he doesn't drink.

Gestes hollers for some of the liquid and a soldier dips a cup in the liquid and throws it at Gestes. The crowd laughs.

"*It is finished!*" Jesus cries out.

As he speaks these words the sun suddenly darkens. It is like twilight but very eerie feeling. Some in the crowd act frightened and start to run away.

"What is finished?" I wonder. Then I remembered the conversation I had with Jesus under the tree when he said, "I must finish the work that I have to do for My Father." His Father is God! Now he can return to his Father and we can go too. That is what he meant. We can go to paradise also!

Gestes, now desperate and realizing there is no other hope, questions Jesus. "If thou be the Christ, save thyself and us."

I push up with my feet and speak back to Gestes. "Don't you fear God? You are getting the same punishment as His Son. We deserve to be here, but Jesus has done nothing wrong."

Jesus turned his head to me and it almost looked like he smiled.

MY NAME IS EZRA *(THE THIEF ON THE CROSS)*

"Lord," I said, "remember me when you come into your kingdom."

With so much effort, each word a torment to his body he spoke to me. *"Truly I say to you, today you will be with me in paradise."*

I cried like a baby. My life on this earth has been such a waste but now I could spend eternity thanking the Son of God.

The earth was dark but inside of me, my soul was at peace.

I could see Jesus now gasping for every breath. He looked up to heaven and uttered his final words. *"Into Thy hands I commend My Spirit."* He breathed his last and his head drooped down. His pain was over.

At that moment the earth began to shake violently. The crowd ran away and a few soldiers flattened themselves on the ground. The rest left.

I was jarred so badly that I am sure my shoulders were now barely attached to my body. I no longer had any feeling in them. What blood I had left started again to seep out all the wounds in my body. To take a breath I had to push up with my feet. I could feel my heart working hard to beat. Every ounce of strength I had I used to breathe. I was still quite aware of my surroundings as my hearing and eyesight seemed surprisingly more acute.

As the sun was coming back out, a few soldiers returned. They whispered something to those remaining and together they walked toward Gestes.

"Crack!" And both of Gestes' knees were broken.

They walked over to Jesus and saw that he was already dead, so a soldier drew a sword and pierced his side.

Slowly they walked in my direction.

"My soul is in your hands Lord," I gasped.

With a smash of a mallet my knees were broke. I thought that I had experienced all the pain a person could bare but this went right through me. I could no longer push up to breathe. I was slowly suffocating. Yet I was at peace. My heart beat once and then stopped, and then

MY NAME IS EZRA *(THE THIEF ON THE CROSS)*

again and then stopped, and then no more.

CYNTHIA THILLET

MY NAME IS EZRA *(THE THIEF ON THE CROSS)*

EPILOGUE

Before sundown, a group of men came with ropes to take down the remaining two men on the cross. Earlier some men had already claimed the body of "The King of the Jews," but nobody claimed the other two. Due to Jewish custom the bodies were not allowed to hang on the cross during Passover so Herod sent these men to take them down.

They went first to the body of Gestes. They tied the ropes around his shoulders and when they lowered the body the spikes tore through the hands and feet. When they got the body to the ground they shuddered when they looked at his face because it had a look of sheer terror. They quickly covered it to hide the hideousness of it.

Then they went to the second man and proceeded to take him down the same way. Diverting their eyes from his face, they slowly lowered him to the ground. When they laid him on the ground, one took a quick glance at his face. To his utter amazement, he had a look of perfect peace.

"Look at his face," he said to the group.

They looked at him with great perplexity.

One finally said aloud what they all were thinking, "I wonder what made the difference in the two men?"

- - - - - - - -

MY NAME IS EZRA *(THE THIEF ON THE CROSS)*

THE OLD RUGGED CROSS

On a hill far away stood an old rugged cross,
the emblem of suffering and shame;
and I love that old cross where the dearest and best
for a world of lost sinners was slain.

O that old rugged cross, so despised by the world,
has a wondrous attraction for me;
for the dear Lamb of God left his glory above
to bear it to dark Calvary.

In that old rugged cross, stained with blood so divine,
a wondrous beauty I see,
for 'twas on that old cross Jesus suffered and died,
to pardon and sanctify me.

To that old rugged cross I will ever be true,
its shame and reproach gladly bear;
then he'll call me some day to my home far away,
where his glory forever I'll share.

So I'll cherish the old rugged cross,
till my trophies at last I lay down;
I will cling to the old rugged cross,
and exchange it some day for a crown.

— George Bennard (Public Domain)

CYNTHIA THILLET